MAN VERSUS HIMSELF

MAN VERSUS HIMSELF

a novel

Erik Keith Benson

iUniverse, Inc.
New York Lincoln Shanghai

Man Versus Himself
a novel

iUniverse, Inc.

For information address:
iUniverse, Inc.
2021 Pine Lake Road, Suite 100
Lincoln, NE 68512
www.iuniverse.com

ISBN: 0-595-28353-5 (pbk)
ISBN: 0-595-65769-9 (cloth)

Printed in the United States of America

For Kharis

CHAPTER 1

I am a handsome man. I am a good man, and yet somehow my balmy blood was running down my arms in vein-like rivers, falling to the sunless sidewalk below. I was just stabbed in the eye by my best friend and business associate. Just last week I had written his annual performance review—he was exceeding expectations. The warm and clammy tip of the stabbing instrument had a handle, and from its feel the handle might have been plastic. Or maybe wood. This unwelcome thing was in my eye. How deep? Was I dying? Several pivotal scenes from a book I recently read (where an epidemic of blindness devoured a town and chaos ensued) flashed like slides in my cerebral cortex.

This eye (the left sibling of a slightly darker blue) was passed down to me in recessive genes—it was last seen calculating in old Manfred's deep sockets. They sat beneath Manfred's heavy lids at the sparsely attended open casket a century prior, and these bottom-of-the-ocean blues slipped under five generations of Bettys before bursting forth once again in full splendor—in my own shallow sockets, on my first birthday.

Although the remaining eye was obscured by tightly gripping hands, I assumed that my blood was sinking hastily into heat-opened crevices and would stain the street until the next rain. The weather report had promised clear skies through at least the end of this week. Cold calmness had effused outwards into my limbs—an accidental blink now would surely magnify the problem. The knife must've been so physically close to the very neurons firing those calm, blinkless thoughts that I suspect they rerouted and defused some key revelations I might have otherwise had. How would I ever find which sections had been neatly sliced out, now gone forever? The stiff gray tissue of my brain had never before experienced anything so machine-refined, so flawless as this simple knife.

I tried not to move. When I inhaled, I could feel the blood in my head cresting and crashing like waves. Breathe shallowly. The only pain I felt was the awareness that the pain would come tumbling in fairly soon. Any minute now. But not yet. What a surreal landscape I was now walking within. I would have a few awkward minutes of reflection and awareness, and then what? Leave the blade in. I knew that man, good old Simon, my best friend and business partner. Maybe I knew him too well. Sometimes two good men could disagree, couldn't they? It didn't automatically make one of them bad.

I did something odd just now. My arm fumbled in my suit jacket pocket, retrieved my camera, extended an arm's length out and snapped a picture of myself: knife pushed to its hilt into my socket, I assumed. Hopefully, the exposed steel wasn't too reflective for the flash. The camera was back in my pocket now. Suede softness, and bloody blood blood.

Here it was. Damn. That hobnobbing, rascally, little man. Ouch. Damn. It was easing off again. Did I really take that picture? Fantastic. I sensed another universe nearby. I'm going to have to frame that. I know just the place for it in my office. And I also have pictures from inside the club with the Mumford sisters on that camera too. Must not lose this. Pat it, it was right there, in the soft pocket, safe. Don't lose my camera, Eliza. I'm going to trust you. I do have a choice. Thanks for the lift, Fred. You guys are always punctual. I must be doing something right.

Ouch. Damn. Rrr. Okay, okay, here it comes, for real. Fig! Yes sir, I will. Just take care of my eye, will you? In the meantime I'll speak however I want.

CHAPTER 2

I must've been in a bloody Willchester bed. My toes met directly with drafts that floated down from the vents. I was hot, I was cold, and the fabric felt dry and unclean. How many worthless employees have soiled these sheets? Don't tell me, doctor, I'm in a bloody Willchester bed. Sure enough. First thing I remembered was the camera. I told the doctor to fetch me Astrid. She'll come in a minute, he said. A minute, bah. Who said I had minutes to give?

He told me what happened, what I already knew. Who needed both eyes, that's why we had two. One's a spare. Despite the somber tone, the doctor found time to utilize the word "lucky" repeatedly, in the context of the stainless steel blade and its navigation through my stiff gray tissue. A few millimeters further, or to the right, or to the left, and I would've been a dead man. I was a lucky man, it was a lucky angle. Yeah, and if I was born a few houses down from where I actually had been, maybe I would've cared. Luck was one of those things that humans had invented in order to justify the weakness, or even absence, of their own decision-making process. I am not a stupid man. I wasn't Mr. Caulfield and I wasn't Hamlet. I wasn't going to barter for a philosophical yet charismatic mind if it came with an equal dose of madness. No matter how well-read and liked I might've become as a result. I knew how books like these ended. I've also read this young doctor's incomplete and inconsistent medical books, and I didn't care which particular booster chair of scientific thought he now sat upon that entitled him to call me lucky. Luck had nothing to do with this or anything else. Now where was Astrid? I had my day to start. I had my city to run.

Astrid, lovely gal, had used her time wisely. She had my tweed suit, my comfortable slacks, my favorite shirt, my best shoes, my strongest cane, and my tallest hat waiting for me. I called Simon (I had no intention of giving him even the satisfaction of feeling he had rattled me), and let him know that the eight o'clock was still on, that I had rented out the board room here at Grey Memorial, and would they please meet me there in forty-five. Bring my presentation. His voice was cautious yet cheerful, the perfect friend.

I took an enormous satisfaction from dressing. It was a man's highest priority to dress himself correctly each and every day. Of course, one could get lost in its labyrinthine philosophies of color, coordination, and style. I wore the same classic tailored tartan tweed style suit each and every day. Three button, center vent suit jacket, V-necked, lower peaked twin pocket, rear adjuster waistcoat, full cut lined trousers, front and rear pockets, button fly, grown-on waist and brace buttons, straight or turn-up bottoms. The shirt underneath was always white. Always white. Each square inch of fabric carried meaning for me. This square inch meant professional. This square inch meant economical. This square inch meant piercingly intelligent. And the meaning of one's suit, carried over decades, worn to elections, board meetings, Thanksgiving dinners, and funerals, melted into one's public persona like brie on a cracker. What it was, exactly, was too subtle for words, and must be absorbed over time. If it were otherwise, I wouldn't have bothered, and instead would've put out an ad on Brad Pitt's forehead. I am a practical man, doubters may refer to this square inch of stretch tweed paradise.

Just as Humbert insisted on his handsomeness often, much to the reader's skeptic tolerance, I was inclined do the same. Only difference, I didn't have the time to bother. Suffice it to say that a handsome man loved dressing, loved combing his hair, loved preparing the angles and planes of his being for visual consumption. How many fist shaking, table pounding board room meetings have I conquered based on looks alone. It would be difficult to know. My left-parted coifery spoke double-time to my mouth's erudite points. The structure of my face resembled Jesus' liberating cross, and had no doubt lent support to every fabricated statistical and unmovable point I had ever made. I was convinced that even the direction of the knots in my Salvatore Ferragamos (the initial folding of laces was done in such a way that the twisting of strings always leaned toward my instep) were crucial to the message that I was trying to make—inseparable even. Anselm Betty was a brand that belonged in every home, a jingle that woke the masses up each morning, and a lullaby that put them to sleep each night. He was man, a plan, a city, and sometimes, a friend. The papers occasionally mentioned that I was perhaps the best friend you would ever meet, and I felt free to quote them from time to time even though it gave me the shivers. I could rattle off reporter-inspired sound bites describing my ways in trite clichés all day, every day, until the end of my days, because I am a sincere man.

Since I was currently lacking the convenience of sight, Astrid gave me her unbiased opinion of my appearance this first of October. Comical, she said. The hat balancing atop a head of wrapped bandages, she said, did the trick. It was eight o'clock.

CHAPTER 3

❀

The oak heels of my Salvatore Ferragamos tapped a morbid tune on the Gray Memorial hallway floor. The tune resonated in the long faux-wooden boards and rang in cheap lamps that had been designed to appeal to the dying. The melody was hypnotizing; I could feel my heart wrapping a heavy cloak around itself as if to prepare for burial, luring me with the promise of a warm reception in soft dirt. I sank my nails into Astrid's thick wool sweater, pulling myself out of simple emotions and into dull analysis. Had Victor and Jack actually been so thoughtful as to take walking sounds into consideration when designing this building? No, Victor and Jack were not that insightful, their steely minds were blind to this level of innovation, and they may even have died long ago.

To counteract these invisible forces, I made a point to exhibit the outward signs of happiness as I counted steps to the board room on floor eleven. When Astrid opened the door, a heavenly chorus of gasps, prepared silences, and rehearsed welcomes presented themselves to my mind as the aural representation of my senior management team.

Chief Scientist Simon pressed his clammy palm to my own with a slap, grabbed my shoulder tightly, and shook me lightly. Yes, I felt quite fine. No, I did not appreciate the Willchester accommodations, but that was no surprise. He was all devilish calm, a kitten playing with its own coughed-up hairball. Arrest him. Chief Algorithms Officer Andreas said donuts and coffee blanketed the table just this way. Chief Technology Officer Jeff and Chief Mathematician Kurt gave their heartfelt condolences and said they had something they wanted to talk to me about when I had a moment. They were undoubtedly missing more deadlines. Most of the senior management team was content to act as they normally did: bored, restless, and predictably quick to rise to argument and bickering. Attempted murder of the CEO was to the Board of Directors as an escalating scuffle on a busy sidewalk was to passers-by.

Astrid established the location of my chair, a flimsy wheeled beast with insufficient cushioning, and maneuvered me into it. Physical objects and employees scrambled into place from this familiar throne, and allowed this business man (sans exposed head) to finally get to business.

Senior Vice President of Media Relations Tara attempted to open the meeting with a smooth yet inaccurate acknowledgment of my headless state, but I waved it away with a personal insult, and after a few moments of silent scuffling, Chief Experimenter Meredith presented results from the Good/White test. This was what I believed myself to be writing down:

> Good/White test ran 6 mo. on two Andom Bay corners: Good and Diedrich, Shin and White. 5 miles apart. 8M instances recorded and examined. 50% in treatment, which tested the placement of a new sign within 5 meters of the walk signal that said "No Jaywalking." The control had no sign. Does the sign have an impact on the frequency of jay-walking? Are our tools sophisticated enough to capture that impact with statistically significant results? Unclear. There were no significant results regarding frequency of jaywalking nor frequency of death on the corner.

I asked for clarification on a couple details that were possibly carved out of my brain the night prior. Was the treatment tested on both corners, or just one? Both. Because the two blocks had similar but not identical traffic patterns, in order to factor out whatever differences there might be, the sign had to be alternated from corner to corner on a daily basis so that the control and the treatment both had equal exposure at both corners, and therefore we could rest assured that there was equal chance of something unique (and statistically damaging) to occur in either the control or treatment. In an ideal world. How about regarding time of day—do we know how people are acting at noon as opposed to rush hour? How about regarding day of week, and month of year? One could imagine that behavior shifts during the week, and during different times of the year, different seasons. No, we do not know that yet. We have the raw data, of course, but not the resources to splice it in that many ways yet. Will we ever have those resources? Doubtful.

This touches upon fundamental flaws in our method. We are building tools that gather enormous amounts of data, but we have not yet found a way to parse that data into all of its various bits of knowledge. Stacks and stacks of computers full of everything knowable under the sun (at least on the corner of Good and Diedrich, and Shin and White) are worthless without tools to extract the valuable cause and effect learnings. We did have some cause and effect data, though, which Meredith was listing now:

> 3 deaths in the treatment, 2 in the control, over a period of six months. Dangerous corners. Could not determine, however, that the control was more or less dangerous than the treatment. So far, the treatment could be 5.2% more dangerous, or 4.89% less dangerous. The number was trending towards being more dangerous, but that was not a number you could rely on.

Why not? It appears that if something was leaning in a certain direction, that that would be useful as an indicator. "Not so," said Meredith. "Statistically speaking, there are no conclusions that you can draw from those numbers—revealing them, even, is deceptive and generally advised against. In any case, do you think it's possible that adding a 'No Jaywalking' sign to the corner could really make the corner more dangerous?"

Maybe it distracted pedestrians, causing them to pay less attention to the traffic. Maybe the fact that people felt they were not supposed to jaywalk made them want to jaywalk even more. Intuition should not sway our interpretation of the facts.

"True. But statistically insignificant results are not facts. Here are the facts then, if you're interested."

> Jaywalkers from north corner: 5% higher in treatment
> Jaywalkers from east corner: -3.1% in treatment
> Total walkers (any type): .4% higher in treatment
> Total cars: 2.1% higher in treatment

This must surely be noise, nonsense. It's preposterous to believe that the sign had this effect on pedestrians. Signs were viewable from every compass direction, correct? Correct.

"And yet, mathematically speaking, these are the results, the facts. However, because our results are based on 95% accuracy, one in twenty facts could be wrong. Again, your intuition is telling you that these results are not valuable, but until we investigate further, and test further, we do not know if there could be some explanation for these results. Anselm, I ask you this, what do you believe to be the more reliable measurement tool, common sense, or statistics based on actual behavior?"

I did not stoop to answering such condescending rhetorical questions. I asked instead to be educated on the mechanisms they were using to gather these numbers.

> 20 Study Boxes at each location, slightly modified from our standard boxes on the Chance network. Each box programmed to capture visual and audio clues and translate them into measurable data. Complex pattern matching algorithms detect the presence of peds, signal light states, cars, accidents. Temp, humidity, and light levels also captured. Data uploaded and backed up in Chance's database every 5 mins.

What went wrong? Something always did.

> Outage on May 28th and June 1st for the control. All results were discarded for those two days. Derek expresses concern.

At this point Chief Treasurer Bob, donning his standard board meeting persona that clashed so aesthetically with his meek one-on-one personality, stuck out this down-turned thumb, blew a raspberry, and poo-pooed the entire experiment. His main points, if I may summarize, included his opinion that unless there were significant results in total deaths, this project's entire business case fell apart. A traffic-induced death cost Andom Bay approximately $10,000 to report and respond to. The cost of research and development for this project rose into the double-digit millions of dollars. In order to justify that expense, it was not satisfactory that we settle for results that did not even have an effect on the level of tens of thousands of dollars. Where was the return on investment? This was not a charity organization, real dollars needed to be lined up on balance sheets at the end of the quarter, and those numbers would be the criteria upon which we were judged by our analysts and investors. Valid, though stale and misinformed, points.

There is a difference between trying to tally up revenue in lives saved and thinking about the real value of a project. The real value, for example, needs to take into account all of the processes that we are developing to run these experiments, as well as the results of those processes. Each experiment we run makes the next one easier and more accurate, and therefore has a definite value to the company. To business nerds, this is what we call the Net Present Worth (NPW), or discounted cash flow. NPW encapsulates the total incremental value that a project will have over its entire lifetime, including any secondary benefits that come about by making all future projects do a little better than they otherwise would. This, I realized, was rhetoric that Bob could or would not understand, and so instead of articulating any of it out loud, I merely told him that this was my company and as long as I was in charge of it we would continue taking an interest in projects like this, even if he himself couldn't pull out each line-item and add them all up into a positive revenue number. He could send disgruntled investors to me. I told him to rest assured—the long-term goal of this company remained the same: not to save lives, not to do char-itable and selfless acts of technology, not to indulge our unrealistic visions of the unforeseeable future, but rather to make money. It was all about money in the end, because even though I did not design it, and had some gripes about it, money was might in this universe, and definitely in this city.

Chief Treasurer Bob accepted this verbally while still disagreeing at heart, and instead of continuing the debate (which, incidentally, was one we picked up and tossed around at almost every meeting, in one incarnation or another), suggested keeping the experiment on until statistical results came back for number of deaths. It may not be important, but it would not hurt. I asked how much it cost to run this experiment, per day. Fifteen hundred dollars. I said, turn it off. Why? We have learned enough. I felt an itching in my skull. I clawed at my head through the proxy of bandages encompassing my head. Side-railed by an itch, I felt the room grow silent. Like flashes from someone else's life, I saw a man whose right eye was carved out, who was sitting in a meeting with his compassionate yet politically-ravenous associates. I tried to imagine the man behind the bandages, the man at the end of his life, falling apart, trying to grasp for stability from the deck chairs. He was pathetic, he had to breathe through tiny holes in the fabric next to his nose and mouth. He was a deformed man, an ugly man, a sick man, an old man, buried under a mound of fleshy illusions. The images were purely emotional and reaction-ary—trapped in fleeting chemicals in my blood, and as such passed like any other biological event would. A few seconds after this daydream, this alterna-tive vision of the present, I felt the sensation fade in my rear-view mirror like potholes on an otherwise well-maintained road. I am competent and creative, insightful and extremely intelligent, probably more so than a vast majority of this world's humans (this was something that I've always instinctually known about myself, and have eighty-nine years of records to prove it), and above all, I had a perfect working model of the causes and effects of political power in my genes, and the confidence to exercise them even now. Everything could, and would, be spun to my advantage.

I listened to the swoosh of a notebook flipped closed, a thud of two dense objects, a brief apology in Simon's reverberato, and extracted the rest of the visual details in my imagination: Simon walked absent-mindedly right into Chief Experimenter Meredith, knocking her lanky frame in the side with his briefcase, meanwhile, she retreated back against the wall and then around the side of the room back to her seat. Simon placed his oily leather briefcase on the podium and exhaled a low grunt. His eye twitched, or perhaps he touched his face nervously, in any case there had to be some hint of his murderous guilt that a trained eye would have picked up. I concentrated on the sound of my beating heart, trying to make it louder, damn it, louder.

The suck of the onscreen projector drowned out the limp static of breathing employees. Like an oboe over strings, Simon's voice entered the melody. He presented a sequence of details that were meaningless on their own, however, when taken as a whole, an image of professionalism, and not only that but also elegance, emerged. He was talking about the Chance 2.0 project.

His speech lacked subjects and objects, and was littered with lingo and mock-religious associations. I knew enough background data to piece the facts together, just barely, before he moved onto the next point. His speech patterns had only a loose relationship with clarity, he was not outlining, he was generating a brand, tying feelings not facts together with the thin rope of metaphor and insinuations. It was familiar, it was my modus operandi. Chance was my company's flagship product: a loosely connected network of one-hundred thousand computers, and if you mapped their relationships to one another, you'd draw up a graph that showed that the Nth most connected computer (for each computer was directly networked with at least 20 other computers) was 1/Nth as connected as the most connected computer. It was modeled after social circles, I've read Milgram and Barabási—this model proved to be the best way to connect the computers together so that it took the least number of steps to pass something from one computer to any other computer. Together these one hundred thousand boxes had enough memory to digitally record every single word ever written, every single song ever played or sung, every single video ever seen—basically every single thing ever thought. Not only could I imagine this happening, but I had proposed a plan, approved a budget, and written up a schedule to do so (if we decided to do so). It was a feasible task, easier than putting a man on the moon. That was interesting to me, but it wasn't the most interesting thing to me. We had bigger plans. Capturing the past had its value, but only in-so-far as it enabled us to understand the present, and even the future. Chance's real kicker was in the interface. It was a tool that provided the buttons, levers, and switches that allowed us to store, manage, combine, summarize, calculate, and distribute enormous amounts of data in an environment that was user-friendly, stable, and most importantly, real time. It told us, at any time, what was happening right now. How many stoplights were green, how many people were in the local bookstore and what were they reading, what was the curve on the graph of time and the number of people at work, at home, in the shopping malls, or in the stadium? Watching the output of Chance's reports, assuming you had the appropriate privileges to be doing so, was like watching the world, or at least Andom Bay, exist. It was the heart-beat, the breath, and the dream all at once: digitally recorded. All reduced to clean, perfect, even and never. At the moment, Chance was only installed in one city: Andom Bay (Little Anhedonia isn't a real city). Our clients were not individuals or corporations, but rather entire cities, and eventually whole nations. That was the vision, at least. Chance 1.0 had been a big step, but it was only a first step. Chance 2.0, Simon's project, doomed from the start, had much larger ambitions than Andom Bay, than Little Anhedonia. All intuitions pointed to its eventual success—for example, Andom Bay, aka Wontchester, aka Don't to your Dochester, Won't to your Willchester, a city only fifteen years old, was one of *Kismet* magazine's Top Ten cities. Why, because of the cascading set of advantages that it inherited from Chance's data. Some people may think that gathering a group of ten people together and giving them the task of making a great city would provide results as quickly as if they were given the task of making a great cherry pie, but it's not. Some tasks, like making a cherry pie, have only one step between the recipe and the result. Making a great city, however, requires ten thousand steps, a recipe with a million ingredients, and a master chef who can keep the whole process in his mind, day and night. The great city emerges from his mind alone. Either that, or the great city is an accident, outside the realm of humans and designs, and nobody can claim responsibility for the result, and nobody can rush in at the last minute and ask for a taste of the pie. I wanted a taste of that pie.

This network was the key. These computers, they talked to one another, could request information from one another or pass it on. They were organized hierarchically. Each box had parents, children, and siblings. They were all Simon's children, I had entrusted them to him. He still reported to me directly, but it was his responsibility to raise them correctly—I no longer had the time or attention to detail that I once had—he had to be there with them during tough times, to stick it through the bad times, and bad times they were. Simon's project was not always his project.

The Chance 2.0 project spun up three summers ago under the leadership of a guy named Albert Strunk. Once titled our Chief Strategic Director, Albert bought low, sold high, and strategized his way to retirement at forty-one. After Albert, the project passed hands like a hot biscuit for about two years between a dozen or so incompetent managers who had no qualms about missing deadlines, and who in fact became compulsively creative in a way that they never were with the actual project in concocting a long list of excuses without any duplicates amongst them: feature creep, lack of resources, failed romance, missing or otherwise departed engineers, micro-management (their own, I assumed), misinterpreted requirements, implementations of features that nobody had asked for, incomplete technical spec, code freezes, and sometimes itching powder.

Simon came onto the project and almost nobody noticed. He was a large man, fairly young, and had a way of stepping on conversations that didn't include him in such a way that people eventually learned to filter him out. Plus, his hair was oily and lopsided on his otherwise unremarkable face. He had an almost obsessive attention to detail, however, and by pushing the schedule for the project out three months, he set aside time to reset expectations on all teams, reeled in the scope, filing a sludge-pile of add-on features that had not been there at the start to a post-launch folder, and got the teams re-energized about a few simple, yet massive, goals. Grow from one hundred thousand boxes to a million. Re-write the interface to allow for easy creation of new accounts, a simple reputation and trust system, and permissions. Make it all wireless. They had monthly meetings with the entire team, and everyone seemed to be on the same page for once during the project's life. Simon had done a commendable job of turning the losing proposition around and suddenly his fat fingers didn't seem to be such a fashion faux pas—it became a symbol of humble, yet competent, management. The era of the ugly manager, at Chance Industries, had begun.

Previous to this meeting, the Chance 2.0 project was considered to be on the path to beta within the next month, and launch a month or two after that in the Andom Bay market. Simon was saying something different now. One of the key advantages of Chance's network was the fact that it was scale-free, which meant that no matter how large the network became, it's overall structure would remain the same. Twenty percent of the boxes would do eighty percent of the work. If we moved from one hundred thousand boxes to a million, we would have two hundred thousand boxes doing eighty percent of the work instead of twenty thousand boxes, but it would remain at that same level of twenty percent. It was designed this way to scale—to allow the easy addition and subtraction of boxes to occur, while also creating a maintainable design that wasn't vulnerable to change. If it became necessary to remove a few boxes for repairs, nobody would notice. Even if fifty percent of the boxes went down, the network would be able to survive (they would have to be a random fifty percent, and not just happen to take down the twenty percent of heavily loaded boxes, of course). It worked much like a brain: resilient and powerful, capable of extremely sophisticated computation, but built out of simple, interchangeable parts. That was the theory, at least. That was the billion dollar investment gamble.

With what I assumed were well drafted, fluctuating charts and graphs, not to mention sliding bullet points and dropping titles, Simon explained the reality of the situation. Maintaining the network had required the uninterrupted attention of 80% of our resources last month, and this number was consistent going back to January. Nothing in particular was more broken than it had been before. Rather, it appeared that it took a directly proportional amount of effort to support the number of boxes that had been deployed. In short (sliding title, mechanical thud), the biological flexibility and scalability that had been written into the business case and requirements doc had not been delivered. We were not scaling correctly. More than that, Simon said, but that emergent artificial intelligence that everyone had been hoping for but never admitting out loud—that wasn't going to happen. Next slide.

Take that back, said Simon, in a retraction that had also been built into the slide presentation, let's not say that exactly, he reiterated, rather, let us say that it looks like it wasn't going to happen (pause) yet.

My eye was spasming under its bed of blankets. I could feel miles of nerve endings flailing about like loose wires, sparking off the back of my skull. My eye socket felt as if it had a ten foot radius and could comfortably hold a potted fig tree. Simon's words, by association, felt weak, forced, and unsatisfactory for a man in his position. Though I may not admit it later, I felt a little angry at him for forcing this discomfort upon me. This wasted eye ball—could it still cry, blink, or dilate? Damn it all.

Simon continued to speak from his colorless podium. Colorless bodies spoke in turn and out of turn around him, people I had long since reduced to intangible symbols of corruption, power, and creativity. They had each been hand-picked from Willchester's dying economy fifteen years ago, shortly after I was fired for a job well done. But now, placed in this new context of not blindness but colorlessness, I could feel their warmth, feel their chill, and even hear sounds born from guileless tongues that fell heavily to the board room table, rolled and rumbled their way outward towards others, slapping the Chief Treasurer, kissing the Chief Algorithms Officer, and spinning weightlessly into the bandaged bowl of my perky ears; sounds devoid of meaning but filling a grand and empty space. Massive, all consuming, empty signifiers in orbit around my soulless imagination. Or thereabouts. People pay good money for that type of serious contemplative investigation of the conscience, you know. I've read Dostoyevsky, I know the underground man, and since I know him, it's impossible to be him. Two people cannot occupy the same space at the same time.

I took out my camera and took a picture of Simon. The camera's gears whirred and spun, like leaves in a small wind tunnel. Souvenirs for my future wife. Lovely little trinkets to remember my day by. The Study Boxes are just a variation on that theme. Data was irresistible. Simon, a man with one hundred thousand cameras, spoke of needing nine hundred thousand more. No matter how much data you captured in a photo or experiment, you always missed most of it. Missed it dearly. Ached for it even. Exactly how many people were saved by the "No Jaywalking" sign? Simon wanted to know. Hell, I wanted to know too. But the ever dividing, splitting, and warping of data taunts the patience. One wakes up one morning, having been stabbed in the eye, and wonders if we're just wasting our time. It's my turn to present.

CHAPTER 4

A shifting cloud of Astrid smells and sounds stood to my left, and I held in my fist a small pen-like object with a red (I recalled) button on the tip. I adjusted the collar of my suit and tried to imagine which face I was making under the bandage.

Uncomfortable silence as my presentation was loaded. Astrid, for each slide, why don't you give me a quick summary of what's displayed. Simon, Meredith, bear with me as there's probably nothing new for you here. This is for those of you who weren't here fifteen years ago when Chance Industries and The Andom Bay Company were founded. Back then we were just one company named Anselm Co, there were five of us, all fired from The Willchester Company for creative differences with Victor and Jack Gray. We formed our own company around which Andom Bay sprouted its wings. The initial five were Chief Scientist Simon, Chief Architect Meredith, then-Chief Treasurer Harold Good, then-Director of Public Relations Una Shin, and myself, CEO. Harold and Una you all know to now be the heads of other businesses in Wontchester, still very good friends of mine. Astrid, can you tell me what's here on the first slide?

"It looks like Tara has a question for you."

Right. Senior Vice President of Media Relations Tara.

"Sorry to interrupt, Anselm. I have no doubt that this will be a very illuminating and educational presentation. We've all come to expect only the most fanatically researched, visually stunning, and relevant presentations from you. However, at the moment I have every newspaper in both Willchester and Andom Bay on hold requesting an update, in fact, any news at all, any reaction or hint of acknowledgement for what happened last night. You were stabbed?

In the eye? Can you spend one moment explaining to me, and perhaps the rest of the people here would care to know as well, how your head came to be wrapped in twenty miles of medical bandages?"

Questions will wait to the end. Thanks. Astrid, can you tell me what's here on the first slide?

"It looks like the first slide is of the original Willchester City Planning offices in downtown Willchester. The building is squarish, with few windows, and looks to be about—"

Twenty stories. Built in 1752 by the old Mendacci family to be a long-stay hotel, but we renovated it in the early fifties when we selected it to be our original headquarters, thanks Astrid. I took this picture many, many years ago, it seems. Willchester, Willchester, Willchester. I loved that city once. I was born there, you know. Sorry. This history is near and dear to me. My heart dances around this story, sometimes playfully, sometimes demonically, always with emotion. Let me get started.

Willchester was one of the first true metropolitan centers in the country. Surely the most progressive in the region. It grew from somewhere around 100,000 residents in 1799 to over five million in 1899. The map of city streets, at first an informal network of connecting dirt roads, grew organically, completely unplanned, during the automotive boom in the early twentieth century. Sure, there were main arteries through the city, but they were not put there on purpose, and therefore they were not put there by design, and therefore they were always congested, clogged, virtually unusable. The rest of the city was the same. Little Italy, the International District, the rich neighborhood, the old person's neighborhood, the safe family area, all of these districts sprung into being without reason. The reason was necessity, but this was not sufficient to ensure that the old person's neighborhood was closer to the hospitals and that the family areas were closer to the malls. Basic city planning common sense was nowhere to be found. Enter the Willchester City Planning company, owned by Victor and Jack Gray, then the two wealthiest business men in this region, who hired the best and brightest minds in city planning to solve the unsolvable problem of Willchester. Unlike Chance, the codebase of Willchester was its streets, its shops, the people themselves, and they were written on the hardware of hills, valleys, lakes and rivers—hardware not easily upgraded. That's the first building we were stationed in, hopeful, unproven, ready for a challenge.

"The Gray Stadium."

A city, in order to grow, needs to be connected. They need to see each other on the sidewalks, in the stadiums, in the theaters. The creative power and intelligence of any group of people is a function of their connectedness. Stadiums, that's one of the simplest solutions to this initial problem. Of course, the stadium was voted down by the public—it was a Catch-22, the people would not vote for a stadium unless they were connected as a community, and the people would not feel connected as a community unless they had a stadium. Victor Gray financed a large portion of this stadium, though it went incredibly over-budget and we did have to dip into city money as well in order to complete it in a reasonable period of time.

"The Underground."

Public transportation. The size of the city had made transportation a very difficult problem, and it was impeding the city's growth. Because Willchester had the luxury of being on fairly flat terrain, the subway was the most obvious answer. We all know this wasn't the case for Andom Bay.

"It looks like this is of the new Willchester City Planning building."

A sailor cannot blow into the sails of his own boat and make it move. You cannot lift yourself up by your own bootstraps. Nor can a city planning company physically exist within the city it is planning. In 1945 we moved headquarters about one hundred and fifty miles outside of the city lines, in an uninhabited hilly region that had not yet been developed. In order to get to work we installed a single line train that traveled between the new headquarters and downtown Willchester. Shortly thereafter, we received funding to begin building this area out, and it became the playground for our most experimental, most idealistic architects and planners.

"A photo of three men, it looks like, hung from a tall tree."

Our work enabled the city to continue growing at an unprecedented pace for another decade. New developments were strategically placed to take advantage of the natural features of the landscape, although there was still chronic bad development happening in the older areas. The people, however, were united. There were youngster sporting leagues, community support groups for reading, religion, and alcoholism, and finally, in 1967, the people united to form lynch mobs. In this case, a Patrick Baker had stabbed a well-known business man in broad daylight, and made off with his wallet which held a few credit cards and perhaps twenty dollars. Immediately, the neighborhood sprung into action and began to independently hunt the man down. Within a few short hours, he was found and handed over to the police (with broken arm). Court proceedings progressed at a standard snail's pace. Several weeks later, in a public hearing, he was scheduled to be tried for assault and battery, resulting in a maximum of ten years in prison. The public was not satisfied. On the way out of the courthouse, a mob of over two hundred local residents seized the man and carried him to a prepared field on the other side of town and hung him. Ecstatic about their accomplishment, someone suggested that they hang two other common prisoners who had recently killed a police officer. Growing more motivated by the second, the group stormed to the city jail, where they were confronted by the jail guard on duty. The jail guard said they would need to get through him if they expected to get into the jail. The mob seized and tied up the jail guard and broke the two criminals out of their cell and hung them next to Patrick Baker in the same field. The next day, the jail guard died from heart failure. In the court case that followed, no single individual could be pinpointed to prosecute. Later that week, the local newspaper printed the following from the coroner's jury:

> "We the jury summoned in the above case find that Patrick Baker, William Smith, and Turner Newman came to their deaths by hanging, but from the evidence furnished we are unable to find by whose hands. We are satisfied that in their death substantial and speedy justice has been served."

"This slide shows the blueprints for several proposed new buildings, I think."

That's correct—shortly after the lynch mobs of 1967 Victor Grey commissioned the building of a new city jail, a new courthouse, and a redesign of existing parks and fields. He was reacting emotionally to the town's coordinated insult of his own governing power, and blamed the city's very design for facilitating the lynch mob's intentions—and in a sense it did. Jack Grey, in the meantime, unbeknownst to us, began pitching the same projects to third-party planning contractors completely unfamiliar with the nuances of the city. Suffice it to say, when we turned our plans in, not only did we discover that a competing set of plans from a small aspiring city planning team from a neighboring town were also present, but we also learned right then and there that our little company had quickly and tragically left the warm spot in Victor and Jacks hearts. Relegated to the cold veins of their outer limbs, we would not be able to succeed in this city for long. Half of the buildings were given to us, and the other half were given to Newco, thus negating any effect the cohesive whole was to have on the city. Newco, as expected, built the tallest, most garish city hall building that was ever imagined—pulling in elements from a dozen different traditions, missing the point of all of them, and in general designing for the layman, the easily impressed, and the ignorant. Think Peter Keating. We were playing Howard Roark. Though, not quite. As professionals, we bend easily. Move the money behind us and we'll usually turn around, if not in complete good faith. Next slide. Oh, yes, I remember this one.

"The Good Willchester Correction Facilities."

I wish I could see it with you. My mind's eye draws a fantastic picture though, layered in the mist and haze of fond memory. Don't tell me, half resort, half entertainment park, this prison was perhaps one of the finest buildings in the city. Anger is a talented muse. The colonnades, the palm trees and video billboards, this was a post-modern correction facility, admittedly perhaps a little too smart for our modest modern city. We put out the question, why must we make all correction facilities cold, dark, and dank? The prisoners are on the inside, but we the virtuous, guiltless and untried have to look at the building all day, don't we? Victor Grey called it a sad parody of a correction facility, and never paid for it, despite our strict attention to the letter and the spirit of his architectural advice. State of the art technology, built to the same disjointed styles as the city hall building, and functional to boot. Harold Good ended up financing this one, hence the name. We took the Greys to court, lost, and were asked to leave the city.

I started crying right there under six feet of bandage. Though the way I cry, it's rather pathetic. My crying sessions last about two-thirds of a second, just long enough for the tear ducts to dispatch enough saline to almost reach my eyes. It's a pre-cry, it should be a warm up for the real thing, but that's it. The emotional cause still roots behind the poor performance, cry bastard, cry! I'm not a cold man, I know this by the things that make me cry: separation, certain commercials, the endings of happy movies, mall music, sometimes just the hint of true innocence in a speaker's voice. In any case, I sped my story up, suddenly claustrophobic.

We turned our attention to Andom Bay, what once was experiment became the foundation of a real lived-in neighborhood with real working people. The terrain was hillier, but we took advantage of the uncovered earth to lay superconducting wires and portable and replaceable computer centers. We wrote our own traffic light software, elevator software, and planned on a mass transit system at the same time that we planned streets and sidewalks. New Urbanism was out, we built a philosophy, history, and codebase from scratch. It was an exercise in self-indulgence, and we whopped and hooted in our own self-made halls. It was rather excessive, but what did you expect from a group of pent up engineers, architects, and mathematicians given an infinite budget and revenge in their hearts?

"The White Building."

Our current headquarters. According to our practice of not living where we build, headquarters was moved back to Willchester, and of course this is where we work to this day, fifteen years later. Andom Bay is a thriving, recognized city, no longer a suburb of Willchester but a destination in itself. And this brings me to my point.

"*Kismet* magazine's article: Top Cities to Live In."

Ten years ago, Andom Bay was nowhere on the list. We are the first city of our kind to make the list in such quick order, debuting at number 9 five years ago, rising to 8 and then 7 over the last couple years, and finally, this year.

Number three. A city that was not even a twinkle in the map's eye fifteen years ago is now the number three city to live in, in the United States. I don't need to punctuate these sentences with exclamation points to emphasize their significance. I only have one gripe with number three, and I'm sure anyone here can guess what that is. Guesses? Yes, number two is Willchester. Let's put an end to that next year. I want ideas next week, a game plan in two weeks, and detailed proposals in my hand in three.

I placed my red-buttoned controller on the table in front of me, and ran my hands along the edge of the table towards the entrance of the board room. I stumbled through the door and held my arms out until a nurse came to help me back to my room. I gave the same presentation to The Andom Bay company senior management team an hour later, and that time didn't tear up at all.

CHAPTER 5

The nurse that walked me back to my room after the second meeting made several wrong turns. I asked her who she worked for. No answer. Then she stopped.

"How are you feeling today, Mr. Betty?"

Like a million billion bucks. Like Anna run over by a train. Like a bloody blooming blossom, and she?

"Do you fear that, with your accident, some of the more unscrupulous members of your companies, naming no names, will start vying for control of the coveted executive chair? How old are you now, Mr. Betty? Almost ninety?"

This wasn't a pack of lions; I was not some alpha geek. I rule the companies I rule for two reasons: I have the vision, and I have the money.

"Wouldn't you say that's a little ironic? To say that you have the vision, Mr. Betty?"

Only if I was a reporter. Simple irony is good for filling the op-ed column on a slow day, but it wasn't going to sell papers, or boost the ratings. Let me guess, KWLT 4 News, you work for a Mr. Daniel Potts, or rather you work for someone who works for someone who works for someone who works for Daniel Potts. Did you know that Danny happens to owe me a favor ever since I gave him that job over thirty years ago?

"With all respect, scare tactics aren't going to work here, Mr. Betty. I haven't broken any laws by taking your helplessly waving arm, nor by navigating you to this isolated corner of the hospital, and least of all by asking you these questions. Remember that it's your duty as a public citizen and CEO of two prominent local businesses to be open and forthright with your friends and shareholders."

We were on the air. I could tell now by the way she spoke not only on her own behalf but supposedly on behalf of the viewer. That all-consuming viewer, to whom The Talent, as they are called, have a direct one-way visual link to twenty-four hours a day, seven days a week, the viewer whom I have to communicate with either through the amateurish talent, or through some other even more inferior means—through a newspaper or television reporter, a press release, a rumor or wild speculation that travels by word-of-mouth on the street. Never on my own terms. This was a problem I had long been peeved about. Simon thought Chance may eventually provide an alternative to this barbarian form of communication, although I have not yet heard it explained in full. I smiled under my bandages, my media smile—an instantaneous, exaggerated, but perfect for television smile. Wasted here. As if flipping through a rolling rack of freshly dry-cleaned tweed suits, I pulled one comfortable caricature out that I felt suited the occasion.

You're right. It's just that I often react sourly towards being deceived, even if it's well intentioned. My apologies for my unprofessional behavior. I solemnly promise that once I receive a full night's rest, I will be a much more pleasant person to be around. I suppose you're interested in hearing about what happened last night? Why I have this ridiculous bandage on my head? And for me to respond to the rumors of political power struggles in the deepest circles of my businesses?

"Yes, if you would, Mr. Betty, we the people of Willchester and Andom Bay would greatly appreciate it."

Has Senior Vice President of Public Relations Tara contacted her yet? Surely she's prepared something for just this type of situation. I stood up straight and adjusted my suit, as if able to see it in a mirror somewhere off camera. Well, it's fairly simple, yes, I was stabbed last night, in my right eye, as I exited from The Yellow Monkey Club. I'm very lucky to even be walking around today, the doctor informed me, I could've easily been killed. God must have been smiling on me. I'm not a young man anymore. Certainly.

"You're still feisty though."

Indeed. This bandage, which some tell me does wonders for my looks, I don't know why I didn't think of it before, will have to remain on for at least another week or so. Who did it? Oh, it could've been anyone. I don't have many enemies these day, compared to perhaps a couple decades ago, sure perhaps a dozen or two that have any real power at all, but any public figure can tell you there's always a chance that something like this will happen to you, it's part of the deal, and I take it in good faith with the rest of my fate, the majority of which has been very much in my favor.

"Come now, you mean you don't feel angry at all for the person that did this to you?"

Anger is an emotion that comes when you cannot act, when something has happened and you're powerless to do anything about it. I have very high confidence in Willchester's crime prevention system (at one point I even played a part in designing it, if you remember, though you may not have been born yet), second only to Andom Bay's own (in my admittedly biased opinion). In any case, I have no doubt that the person responsible will pay ten-fold for their actions. Meanwhile, I still have one good eye they tell me, which I assure you is plenty, and I can still try to make myself useful around here. I have businesses to run, an election coming up, and a couple cats at home that are probably waiting anxiously for my return.

"You're an amazing man, Mr. Betty. Truly inspiring. On behalf of the staff at KWLT and the people of Willchester, I wish you a speedy recovery."

Thank you.

"Cut. You weasel. You old dog."

Can I ask you a favor? I pulled out my camera, wrapped my arm around the woman, held the camera in front of us, and snapped our picture. I'd like this one to be on the cover of the *Andom Bay Times* tomorrow.

CHAPTER 6

She pushed me in the direction of my wing of the hospital and fell away into silence. It wasn't long before another attendant of the hospital found me and cooed and baby-talked me back to my room, where I sat down in a stiff chair and slept for a good ten minutes. During that time I had a dream of an empty dirt field where nothing happened, but everything was in order.

I woke up when a nurse knocked on my door. She said I had two visitors, and would I like to see them?

It was Victor and Jack Grey's voices in sing-song unison. Victor placed a heavy bundle of lilies in my arms and Jack gave me his sincere condolences. I wasn't dead yet, though it made no difference to them. I thanked them for the flowers and asked the time. I told them I had another meeting to go to in a couple minutes, but I appreciated their coming. They should contact Astrid and arrange a lunch for us sometime next week. When they were gone I inhaled deeply, and let it out slowly. One, two, three, four. I called Astrid.

The Board had passed an impromptu amendment to the law which decreed that all City Council meetings take place within the city limits (and in particu-lar inside the Murphy Building). It was rushed through during the first couple minutes of an emergency meeting this morning in accordance with the guide-lines set forth in Rule 0231. The amendment added a flexibility clause that allowed the City Council meetings to be occasionally rescheduled to take place outside of the city limits—and it was immediately put to use by designating the next meeting to take place this afternoon at Grey Memorial. It was their only option since I would have refused to be absent, and would've refused to have it cancelled. The Board of Directors in Andom Bay was a group of eleven individuals in the city who either held important office, or ran important businesses. Most of the law-making that fell under the city's jurisdiction took place in these meetings, in a forum that was as progressive and experimental as any other aspect of the city. It was designed and initially implemented Boris Schuber, philosopher and friend and honorary member of the Board (though not an eligible voter). He called the initial law set the Schuber Laws, and they were a list of thirty-two laws, sixteen of which were immutable laws, which could not be changed, and sixteen of which were mutable laws, which could be changed according to the laws regarding law-change. From the initial set, law number 0002, an immutable law, stated, "Any immutable law can become a mutable law if the change is voted on unanimously by all eligible voters." Every law, therefore, could in theory be changed, given an appropriate percentage of voters felt that it should. At a City Council meeting, new laws were proposed by each member in turn, alphabetically by last name according to one of the laws, and voted upon. An eligible voter is any voter who was an eligible voter at the end of the last meeting, who was also present for the current meeting. Votes that passed were entered into the Andom Bay Book of Laws, in the state that they were voted upon. Copies of the Andom Bay Book of Laws were made at the end of every meeting and made available to any citizen of Andom Bay for $15.99 + $.01 per page through a lightning printing press. As of today, the Book of Laws was fairly slim, running a little over two hundred and fifty pages. The Great Purge a few months ago was largely responsible for its current state, as that had removed most of the obsolete and invalid laws in one grand sweep and clean. Prior to that the book had been over three thousand pages, and the number of amendments and references had been greatly impeding the ability for new laws to be approved and integrated without great effort. What remained after the purge, a proposal which I had invented and implemented after two years of research (a sign of just how unmanageable the laws had become), was an incredibly flexible, portable, and useful book of laws that had no known loopholes, and which was able to handle new situations (like the relocation of the board meeting) in a timely and elegant manner. If only this book had been around in the days of Patrick Baker, perhaps the mob never would've had to take justice into their own hands. On the other hand, if there had never been Patrick Baker, perhaps this book never would've been written. Fanciful daydreams were distracting me from finishing this phone call. A few minutes later, I hung up, and called the doctor in.

I told the doctor I was a reasonable bearer of pain, by which I meant I didn't complain about pain unless it was especially noteworthy, but this was just getting ridiculous. I did not know how to put it exactly, I told him, but the pain was quite substantial. Who knew an eye could demand so much of my moment-to-moment attention? It was as if this single organ had launched a broad campaign throughout my entire body, unloading considerable pain packets originally designated for the eye onto my knees, shoulders, etc. The result, it hurt to walk, to lie down, to move my toes, to talk, even to think. I asked the doctor if there was anything he could do—I was open to any and all drug options, but would not permit being confined to my room. He gave me a plastic container of a new prescription, instructing me to take one whenever I was in unbearable pain, and that was the most he could do without hooking me up to a morphine drip. I did not want to wheel anything around either. I offered the good doctor a job in Andom Bay, where his professional talents would be better appreciated, at double the pay. He said he would think about it and gave me his card. We parted rather amicably, my first pill already taking effect.

I'm not sure if most people did this, but I was constantly fine-tuning my mental threshold for the noticing of change in my environment. To me it seemed that most people didn't pay attention to things like the first gray hair, or the squint it takes to focus on the signs you used to be able to see. Instead, it may take fifty gray hairs, or the doctor at one's yearly optometrist appointment before most people noticed changes, before the rusty wire of attention was tripped and knowledge was passed to the consciousness. When Victor and Jack had outsourced projects to Newco, I knew that I should've noticed something much earlier than that. It could've been a twitch in their eye, a letter that was returned a day late, or a cancelled lunch date. Or it could've been a newly painted car—the symptoms did not always directly relate to the disease, but there were always symptoms if you knew what they looked like. Stephen King wouldn't have missed that detail, so why should I? Ninjas and detectives responded to slight shifts in temperature, and other subtle clues that the average man could not, and I envied them. What I noticed just now, as my heels clip-clopped their way down the hallway, same old ditty, was that my threshold for noticing change itself had changed. In other words, I was not noticing things that I knew I should. KWLT's news talent shouldn't be the first to tell me of power struggles in my own company. I had been aware of struggles, of course, since day one, that's not what I'm saying. In fact, it was such struggling that I lived for, I practically invented it, but I knew that I hadn't been paying proper attention to the nuances recently and I might have already missed a crucial change in the environment that would lead to my eventual downfall. The fact that Simon had executed an eyeball stabbing so flawlessly and in such a way that he was still comfortable sitting next to me and presenting his failing project to my face was telling. The fact that Victor and Jack could make their way past all my defenses and come to my hospital room to offer flowers—despite being two decades deceased—something was definitely different, changed, perhaps broken. I needed to wake up the watcher in me, to pay extra attention in this coming meeting and beyond, if I expected to make it through to see my city beat out Willchester in next year's article. Wake up, sleepy head, wake up.

Eleven ghostly members of the Andom Bay board of directors gathered around the table as Simon set up the voting hardware that we used to cast anonymous votes. The standard set-up was that we each had tablet PCs through which we voted on a secure network, communicating directly to Chance who returned the result of the vote to every voter at the end of a round. Today the network was malfunctioning—the tablet PCs could connect to it, but the secure server which we normally connected to was down inexplicably. Security here was not a light or simple issue, requiring several steps of encryption to ensure that no one individual had a way to access votes, and after several hectic minutes of listening to the rumblings of discontent coming from Renold, Kenneth, and Maxine, I proposed using the traditional pen and paper method to record votes, and that this proposal be voted upon using an open vote, which didn't require the fancy tablet PCs. The bandaged bandit's idea was passed with six verbal yays and the regularly scheduled meeting was under way.

Kenneth Mealy, owner of twelve local restaurants and bars, put forth the first proposal for consideration: new awnings for all local businesses in preparation for the coming holidays, with a small percentage of space reserved for controlled advertising. New awnings will be offered on a volunteer-only basis for all businesses within the eligible districts. All volunteers will be granted a certain number of free advertising spots on other store banners in proportion to the amount of business they refer using their own awning. Slips of paper were handed out to the eleven board members, which we marked according to preference. The votes were then gathered together and tallied by Harold (who was sitting to Kenneth's left). Five votes for (Kenneth, Daniel, Ruth, Maxine, and Renold), six votes against (Simon, Harold, Una, Trevor, Eliza, and myself). Voting was anonymous to everyone but Harold, true, and the names are simply my best guesses, but trust me, they're correct. Proposal rejected.

Simon, our representative from Chance Industries, puts forth the following proposal for consideration: an amendment to Law 0205 that states that the privacy of legal citizens prevents any third party from collecting data about them that can be sold, rented, or given to any third party, nor can it be used in the court of law without their explicit written or recorded verbal consent beforehand. The proposed amendment will alter this law so that the definition of legal citizen applies only to individual citizens, and not to anonymous groups of twenty or more. In the cases of groups of citizens greater than twenty, data collected about that group at large can be entered into the collection of evidence for a particular relevant court case, as well as sold, rented, or given to third party businesses, as long as any data that could be used to link anonymous members of the set back to individual citizens was omitted. Kenneth counted the votes. Six votes for (Simon, Harold, Una, Trevor, Eliza, and myself), five votes against (Kenneth, Daniel, Ruth, Maxine, and Renold). Again, I have no tool, other than a keen understanding of the members and my own intuition to know for certain that this accurately predicted who voted for what, but my keen understanding and intuition were rarely wrong.

Daniel Potts, CEO of Region Media which owned KWLT in Willchester and KABA in Andom Bay, good friend and fine adversary, put forth the following proposal for consideration: "Anonymous voting is broken, fine fellows, so broken in fact that I believe I would be able to predict not only the outcomes of the following two votes without error, but also each person's specific vote. My hunch, though I would not be so proud as to presume I could prove the subtleties of this process, is that there may be a subtle system of visual and audible clues that inform vote suggestions to others who follow those suggestions, and therefore, by controlling the majority of voters, effect the outcome of any proposal. My proposal, therefore, is this—specifically designed to be perhaps a little frivolous, in the hopes that the powers that be do not shoot this down without giving me a chance to play my game: if this proposal is accepted, during the two rounds that follow this vote (meaning, therefore, your vote for this proposal will not be included in the two votes) I will submit along with my regular vote a list of names who have voted for the proposal in question. I ask that you too keep a record of your vote for the next two rounds. At the end of these two rounds, we will compare these two lists and see if I've guessed correctly. In essence, I'm asking that the next two votes be open, not anonymous, though they will act as if they were anonymous until after the fact. My only request is that there be no breaks between now and the next two rounds, for fear that my prediction skills may not be robust enough to see through a coordinated effort against it, if such a thing were allowed. If and only if I've guessed one hundred percent correctly, a second proposal, which I will write down on this piece of paper now, and possibly reveal later, will be voted upon. In exchange for the two correctly guessed outcomes, this proposal will start out with a two point advantage in the polls. After the second proposal passes or fails, if it is voted on at all, this proposal and all record of it will be purged from the Book of Laws." Crunching leather indicated that Daniel had sat back down, and was ready to tally the vote.

CHAPTER 7

Objections were made by members of the board who cited conflicts with previous laws, but I knew that Daniel had created a beautiful, elegant, disastrous proposal, and that it could mean the end of an era for our posturing and hand-gesturing alliance. Not, mind you, because his plan as conceived would actually work, but because of an almost imperceptible message sent forth from the deepest recesses of the game that power had changed hands, and that if I didn't recover quickly, my king would be taken in precisely four moves. The only problem (for Danny boy) was that I saw the game even further out and saw something even more beautiful (for myself). Rather than fight Danny, I could see that only by bending in the wind would I survive, perhaps coming out of it at the conclusion as a different thing than I was today. I was breathing heavily, and my nostril's exhales created warm tide pools of energized molecules within my cast-covered face as it ricocheted off the bandages. I refused, like any real gentleman, to sit with my mouth hanging open, a facial function reserved solely for the befuddled and confused, while I preferred agitated nose breathing with eyebrows (not seen here) raised.

A folded scrap of college-ruled paper cupped in my right hand, I used my left to send one message onto the paper and another onto my peers. The five men and women in this room who operated businesses and/or credit cards and lifestyles on my account would vote for this proposal, believing that I too would vote for the proposal—for what other intention could I have? I relied on a fundamental illusion of the self: the transactions of others were never as complicated as your own. If I had actually believed in this tempting illusion (distinct from believing that it was an illusion, and still indulging it), the illusion that my own motivations were actually much more subtle and convoluted than my peers', I would be as big a fool as the others in this room appeared to be. Better to subscribe to the much more optimistic and reaffirming notion that others were as complex, unpredictable, and paradoxical as oneself (despite all evidence and instinct to the contrary) than to be forced to live with a self with no modesty, no capacity for true imagination, one with no ability to conjure up a magic land where in fact they were not the king of all things. I am a megalomaniac of such high order that I conveniently place between myself and my megalomania a series of self-diminishing one-way mirrors that make me appear smaller than I actually am, and others to appear larger.

The all-consuming empty signifier that I was given at birth (for we were all given one, like little towels handed to one at the entrance to a spa) was an incredibly tricky environment, but once mastered could provide endless entertainment. I say endless! The imagination, henceforth referred to as Agent, navigated the all-consuming empty signifier, henceforth referred to as the Landscape, searching, presumably, for a way out: an edge, a wall, a door. Every door, however, led back in. The trick to this game, for every game has a trick, was to realize that the Agent was the Landscape, the Landscape was the Agent, and for all practical purposes, a portion of the Landscape was navigating itself by itself, like a dream protagonist who imagined himself dreaming within his own dream. The dreamer, dream, and dreamed were all one imagination, the imagination had imagined itself within itself, and every exit it could imagine was still constrained by the fact that it had to be imagined by the imaginer before it could be found.

And this was how I planned to play the game of the Book of Laws today. I would let Danny's proposal win by a six to five margin, the deciding vote being my own, which would then be a trivial matter to staging it as a traitorous vote, giving me sufficient license to eventually fire my hobnobbing, rascally, best of friends, Simon. At this point, as if perfectly timed, introducing a random element to the voting structure would actually prevent Simon from doing what I know he was planning on doing very soon anyway: switching sides, thus giving the opposing minority the one person advantage required to make it the majority. I believed myself to be the better player when it came to surfing the Book of Laws while it was in a state of flux. Laws about laws were always my favorite, a self-indulgence I usually refrained from, as some might say I have a little Gödel in me, a little Derrida, a little Foucault, a little blah-dee-blah.

When Simon counted the votes, however, I exasperatingly (since it seemed so obviously wrong to me) requested a recount. He re-counted a number which seemed impossible to conceive even as a possibility: ten votes for, one vote against. I suspected trickery; a flock of panicked birds flew through the claustrophobic veins and arteries of my mind, upsetting biorhythms that had been in stability for years. Stabbed again, this time in the back. Ouch. And damn. The proposition passed, I calmed down, and I tried to piece names together that would fit this scenario, as it seemed that the others would assume from the evidence (if I didn't know contrary-wise by the actuality of my own vote) that I had voted against it and everyone else had voted for it. The last hurrah for the one-eyed ruler, they might think. All good things must end, they might say behind my back, even Rome fell, what goes up, must come down, the bigger they are, the harder they fall, these and a dozen other clichés rattled through my stalled skull. I pushed the nightmare away, numbers and statistics could be so insidious and hateful sometimes, and popped another pill.

Una Shin, CEO of Handsome Advertising, a lovely woman to whom I was once was engaged (at least by my story), was always a delight to hear enunciating consonants and vowels of any flavor. As she spoke, she brought to halt my apocalyptic interior monologue, and her voice came into mine ears as if by light-winged, trumpet-punctuated, delivery from the angels: refreshing, clean, and, as always, noble and intelligent. Were it not for she and the Mumford sisters, my life might've been one devoid of romantic love (and, coincidentally, heartbreak) entirely.

She proposed the following in her trademark style: resurrecting the rejected vote for Kenneth Meany's advertising network and combining it with Simon's accepted proposal to sell aggregated citizen information, into an über advertising network that was founded on aggregated citizen information. Specifically, Chance Industries would be called on to put to use our recently compiled database of retail business connections ("Customers who shopped at this store also shopped at," and the reverse, "Customers who shopped at the following stores also shopped at this store") by initially investing in Handsome Advertising and financing the creation of one hundred prototype street corner video advertising billboards to be installed around the city. Each business within two city blocks of any particular billboard would be invited to purchase a standard advertising package that promised placement on the billboard's rotation of advertisements. In addition, all billboards that had primary businesses that were similar to their own would feature secondary advertisements, still TBD design-wise, letting customers know that if they liked this or that local business, they might also like this or that other business that's just a short jaunt across town. Just how many secondary billboards your business would appear on would depend on an algorithm that factored in Chance Industries' business correlation data, the physical distance between the two businesses, and the number of advertising dollars that the secondary business has provided to be advertised alongside the primary. The more businesses paid, the weaker the correlation had to be between themselves and similar businesses for them to be advertised alongside them, and the further the businesses could be. Those correlations had been found to follow Zipf's power law, meaning that there would be a fairly low bar of entry to the network, letting you gain exposure on a fair number of billboards for a low cost, but any business that attempted to spread their ad across the entire network of businesses would spend a fortune in doing so. It was a win-win situation for businesses, for customers on the streets, and for the city. However, because it required the coordination of hundreds if not thousands of businesses, as well as some third-party to invest in the infrastructure and data, this was an opportunity that no other city had taken. We had the platform, and that has made all the difference. Christmas in Andom Bay could be one of the greenest ever. Una's voice quivered with childlike excitement, as hands began to rise with questions.

Eliza asked that references to the specific businesses of Chance Industries and Handsome Advertising were deleted from the proposal according to Law 0538 which stated that no proposal may be constructed to specifically to benefit an individual or business. The proposal was therefore revised to omit the names and substitute them with "third party content providers" and "advertising agency," leaving open the possibility that any similar business may offer these services, should one suddenly arrive in town and set up shop overnight.

Ruth asked how the revenue would be split up amongst investors. Should not some of the proceeds go to help support local non-profits who perhaps did not have the means to compete in this environment, the Church (of which she was residing pastor) for example? Would any business be allowed to participate? Even, say, some of the more sketchy bars and adult establishments? Also, she foresaw that some businesses would not appreciate having other businesses advertised alongside them, as it hurt branding and broke down much of the intended effect of ads designed around a hypothetical assumption that they were the sole entry in their category of product. Finally, it might be a good (i.e., revenue generating) idea to build in a way for businesses to suppress secondary ads alongside their own for an increasingly more expensive percentage of the time.

I lost interest in the ensuing debate as I was torn between taking advantage of the real benefit that this would bring to Chance Industries—this proposal had, I know, been long in coming—as that would strengthen Simon's platform as well, my other option being to shoot myself in the foot to save the leg, and also take an obvious step in thwarting Daniel's guessing game. When articulated, however, the choice was simple. I held the paper in my right hand and scrawled with my left, drew alongside my vote a picture best I could of a queen of hearts which probably came out more like a child's rendering of a ball of worms. On the other sheet I drew a king, with a gun to his head, and the opposite vote. I am an unscrupulous man, one who only played by the rules because the rules permitted rule breaking. And I had made the rules that way on purpose. The proposal passed, again ten to one, and papers were shifted, filed, stamped, folded, and filed again.

Eliza's proposal passed over me like a damp cloud, whatever it had been about failed to trigger the wire required to gather my attention. My brain was quickly being depleted of the chemical that cared. Oh yes, the elections. We had two candidates, one running in Andom Bay, the other in Willchester. Victor and Jack were sponsoring the other two, and also had one in each city. Our women were professional, beautiful, brilliant, and dangerous, I do remember that. Their platforms, primary issues, and plastic faces failed to interest me, though I knew they had captured my full attention a mere twenty-four hours prior. We would do what we had to do, I trusted. Maybe the Council will have succeeded in ousting me and dumping me into an unattended ditch by then and I would be free, free of this circle of betrayal, this square of imprisonment, this triangle of logic and power. I should not be letting myself degenerate to this extent, that was plainly obvious, but it was a Catch-22: I would only be able to pull myself out of this state if I cared, however, since the state was explicitly one of not caring, I would not pull myself out. At the same time, knowing myself well enough to know that I would soon care again, even though I could not conceive of such a time, I could feel a sharp kicking in the back of my mind telling me to wake up, so there must be a part of me that was still alive under all these drugs, these bugs, these magical rugs.

I voted against it, though my short term memory could not recall exactly what I was voting against. The proposition lost, six to five, according to the standard alliances, though I had not made the appropriate signs for it to do so. I stood up, excusing myself, for I knew that I was not feeling well and should not be representing myself here. I was only hurting myself by staying at this point. Daniel urged me to stay a few minutes longer, while he revealed his guesses and the answers. Paper exchanged hands, corners were lined up on the table, hieroglyphics analyzed for meaning, everything folded into a giant origami crane. Astrid came in, suddenly upset about something, and carried me out. Last thing I remember of that meeting was a snapshot of Daniel and Simon talking together with arms around each other, and the thud of an exploding bomb in the building next door (though, upon recollection, that may not have happened).

CHAPTER 8

My body, the doctor told me, was not healing itself as it should. He did not mention why. I told him I would hold a meeting with my immune system and offer to completely revamp its headquarters building if it would only complete this one project on schedule. He didn't laugh. I reminded him that I was the one in unbearable pain here, and should not have to be the one to supply the humor at this meeting. I imagined Astrid, at least, keeping a knowing smile on for me, standing behind the doctor.

Doctor, how long have I got?

Doctor, what about my babies?

"You have no children, Anselm."

I'm dying, Doc, but I haven't yet lost my mind. I know that I've got two chubby little girls who at this very moment are sleeping soundly in their beds at home. The doctor (was I seriously considering hiring this guy in Andom Bay?), may have looked nervously at Astrid, consulting with her about what to say, how to phrase it politely. Of course I was just playing with him, and I let him know by lightly punching his knee—except I missed and slammed my knuckle in the bed's railing. He may have been on the other side of the bed for all I knew…my hearing was not providing me with much directional information as far as the sources of these voices went. Perhaps I was not a fully reliable narrator at this point, I guess he had some reason to be worried about me. My eye consumed my soul. I sat on the lip of my eye, kicking my legs into the lava below, then had a dream about being in the hospital with a humorless doctor, as I tried to lighten the mood with ineffective jokes.

CHAPTER 9

❀

I got the dirt field often during the frequent slipping in and slipping out of what I believed at first to be a nap but may have been a coma. The dirt field was easy, it was obviously a dream object, one that possibly represented my longing for a time before Andom Bay, before Willchester, when the valley and neighboring hills were still outlined in the soft malleable crayon of Mother Nature rather than the inerasable semi-permanent marker of men. That, or it could be a longing for the sweet kiss of the grave. I wasn't willing to say confidently that it was one or the other. Most of my mental resources in this rather inconvenient coma were devoted to labeling things as they came to me. The tiny wicker chair I pulled out onto the sidewalk in front of Café Fugue and sat in as I watched the citizens of Andom Bay stroll, gallop, and catwalk by, that was a dream object based on a real object. That particular chair being my favorite artifact from Law 1320 which stated that every café and restaurant (except those that applied for a waiver) must have at least three tables on the sidewalk, as that encouraged people watching both from inside the establishment and outside. People watching, according to Jane Jacobs, noted city planner, Queen of the Feet People, was a simple health precaution for a city, likened once to buttoning your shirt from the top. It was just good taste. Plus, my favorite show was always on, the commercials did not interrupt the flow of the program, and the actors were cheap.

The conversation detailing the precise location of my will—I think that was real. Real because I did not see their faces, nor their bodies, and instead, as their hushed and urgent discussion unfolded rather slowly and painfully, I blurted out, "Check my files, look for a Mr. Skip Winters. He'll help you out. Though I think he's in Florida until first thaw." The only reason I'm not positive this was real was because I counted voices that, were I in a less coherent state, I might attribute to my three evil stepsisters: Gracie, Julie, and Katherine. Weren't they dead? Maybe not, maybe not indeed.

There was a lot of family in the mix, more than I might have otherwise guessed, since I had not thought about them for perhaps a few decades. Mom and Dad Betty, of the original Manfred Betty clan that chugged up the coast however many hundred years ago and sent the first words back to the narrowly escaped industrialized death pit of a village proclaiming the righteous and benevolent land of milk and honey that they had discovered. Rich in lumber, packed with untapped resources, the great-great-great-great-great-grandchildren of these pioneers now owned eleven of the twelve tallest buildings in Willchester, sixty story office buildings being dwarfed by one hundred story office buildings, all rented to the highest bidder. They looked over the city at night and counted their toys. We lived in a little golden box at the top of Betty Tower. I've always insisted that despite the fact that all of my toys were a thousand times better than yours, my childhood was just as painfully dull.

But now, forward to present, you know, where I'm dying, trapped in an unimaginative coma, perhaps aging at ten times dream clock time—I get a golden box in my pudgy hands. A prototype, I think. Simon's golden box, although I don't remember seeing this in the real world. It's not a Rubik's Cube, not a replica of my childhood home, not a Study Box, but something smarter, better. Maybe Simon had been in my room telling me of his evil take-over plans and had mentioned this Golden Box to me, not thinking I was awake; which I wasn't, but my subconscious had absorbed the fact and, like a faithful insider, whispered it to me in my sleep. In any case, I labeled it a dream object, connection and meaning unknown.

That silly dirt field, again.

Oh, now the stainless steel pocket knife, lodged in my eye socket. I labeled this as a real object, due to the physical marks still present in my skull. The knife, even if it had since been extracted, could be defined as the negative space of my brain, and the negative space of the knife, everything else, was me.

Victor and Jack Grey were visiting me, and their steely minds reminded me of the knife, and their constant flowers reminded me of my parents. Victor and Jack Grey, two bulbous heads attached to one monstrous body, were speaking with my parents, in my hospital room. They were friends, you know. Of course you do. They had found my will, stashed in the one place they hadn't thought to look. Lucky me, the whole family was there, discussing my constant distance, my odd childhood, my wild successes and devastating failures, and they were chomping on something crunchy, cafeteria carrots, or maybe hospital hot dogs.

Anselm was a business man. He was a thinking man. He was a beautiful child. He was a hateful young man. I was awake! I could wiggle my toes, move my eyebrows, I could speak to them right then if I so desired, I was a mere few feet from their cold dead bodies, and yet this seemed more unreal than the dirt field, than the Golden Box, than the bomb next door. I let my soul sink back, intending to smuggle myself onto the first boat to la-la land, land of Cerberus, Hades, and Persephone, land of harps, Thanksgiving feasts, white togas, dead pets, and childhood crushes. Because this was killing me.

But no boat came, I think it was this damn Willchester bed. I sat up and tried to remove the bandages from my head. Hands fell upon me and restrained me, oh God Anselm, typical Anselm, that trickster, always spying! I grabbed for the walkie-talkie that connected me to the nurse's station: "Take this bloody bandage off my head!" I had been gypped. I never even got the tunnel with the light.

CHAPTER 10

Now they were saying I was not in fact going to die, that I had made a miracle turn-around recovery and it was even fine for me to go home if the fancy hit me. They didn't bother with trying to justify their oversights, their faulty records, labyrinthine causes, and Babylon effects—why bother, it would've been foolish. They do hope the staff here at Gray Memorial was warm, friendly, and kind. Pleasantries ad nauseum. It was a true Willchester experience, thank you. And thanks for the candy, doctor. They didn't realize I was allergic to the candy, and had almost killed me with their sugar-coated pain-softeners. Oops!

The debriefing with a police investigators went smoothly (though they looked exasperated, taking their job so seriously). It was simple, they insisted on information from me and I refused to give it. No names were named, no friends were blamed. This was not a cop story, my coma had made that clear. This was a man versus man story, and old versus young story, a me versus them story. It was mine and I intended to keep it.

We took the choo-choo back to my abode, taking the single thin tunnel out of town and onto the open valley and then climbing slowly the pre-hills of Andom Bay, and in that mode I made my humble return to sanity after a ninety-six hour vacation, my only souvenirs consisting of a canvas bag over my head and a flimsy doctor's slip with instructions in six languages (not including braile, the only one that would've actually been useful) on how to remove the bag and administer my fancy pirate's patch once I was in the comfort of my own home.

Mom, Dad, and the three evil stepsisters took a helicopter, and I shared my train voyage with Astrid and Simon, who wasted no time in catching me up on the story in which I was slowly being made a secondary character.

Daniel guessed correctly for the two votes as expected, despite the fancy trick I tried to pull with the Queen/King swap. The proposal he then made, which passed six to four, nicknamed Minority's Hope, involved administering a number of randomization elements to the voting process. Chance would be programmed to follow the following logic after receiving all votes, and prior to delivering the tally back to the Council: every vote in a round will have a set "chance to flip" usually set to a fairly low number like 1%. This means, after a vote was cast, Chance's randomization engine would roll the electronic die and, if it returned a one (it having presumably one hundred sides), then the yay would turn into a nay, or a nay would turn into a yay. Otherwise, it would stay the same. Every vote in the round had a chance to flip as set by the voter between one and ten percent. In addition, Chance would keep track of certain other factors such as the number of times you have voted this way in a row, the number of times you have voted this way on propositions by this particular person, and whether or not all of the votes from all of the people could be found to follow any consistent pattern. Each of these patterns, when detected, would increase your vote's chance to flip. The purpose of this system was to ensure that no one voter could be entirely sure at any time how the other voters initially voted, and therefore could not exert pressure on any individual voter (either monetary or social or other) for not voting as they were instructed. Some votes, it will turn out, especially close votes, may end up going to the minority some of the time—if some of the majority were flipped by Chance. Over any period of time, however, the effects of this proposal will remain neutral on general trends, and will have the least chance of effecting votes that are controlled by a large majority. This proposal would officially be incorporated into the next City Council meeting.

A harmless proposal, in my eye, though I never would've voted for it. The mysterious allure of randomization had always had a strong pull on me, and a city ruled by randomization (true randomization being a truly difficult piece of software to write) could not be an evil one. Evil, of course, being the poor man's word for rich. I'd had a stranglehold on the Board of Directors for so many years that perhaps it did not yet occur to me just what was being destroyed here. Years of handshakes and finger tapping, the long evolution of subtle social pressure using tardiness and forgetfulness when votes were not cast to my whim by men and women whom I controlled. Perhaps if I had been given enough time to dwell on it, still under the illusion of having a grasp on "the way it once was," I would have made a few budget cuts and dinner dates and have had the entire affair back under my control within the week, but Simon segued into the next order of business so smoothly and professionally (he must have had a wise mentor) that I quickly woke up to the fact this was just the beginning, and I probably should not become too smug just yet.

After Eliza's election proposal came another dim-witted proposal from Ruth detailing conditions for my temporary leave of absence from the Board on account of my declining health (should I even survive, which they understood was not entirely certain). This way, they reasoned, with certainly no thought of themselves, that I might be given time to heal and regain perspective. In the interim, Ruth too would volunteer to step down temporarily from the Board in order to keep the number odd and the vote pure, as she had business to deal with in Albania that she had been putting off for too long already.

Simon held a private meeting with the senior management Team at Chance Industries the next day, as I was possibly labeling knives and forks like a newborn baby in my coma, and explained my situation to the senior members who all agreed that after all my years of hard work, I deserved a month or two of rest at my home if and when I emerged from my coma. My services would be needed again in the office when? Never, Simon said, not unless I wanted to come back, and at that point the capacity of the return could be negotiated.

My family had flown in from all five corners of the globe shortly thereafter, I'm told, promising to handle all funeral arrangements should their hopes be realized, and of course sorely disappointed when they discovered that this world was still longing for me in a humorless and sort of sarcastic way.

The Andom Bay Company, the small company from which everything preceding had once sprung, and possibly the only group of people who did not think me completely useless just yet, sent Astrid a letter yesterday saying that they were praying for my health, and that President Miller would water my plants during my absence but hoped for my speedy return lest the company crumble to the ground in my absence.

In the meantime, as I learned when pulling up to my home on a hill, I discovered that my evil stepsisters had made sure that my entire house was ripped asunder so that I might feel as alienated in my own home as possible. My old bed was lifted via crane out my large bay windows and replaced with a canopied affair and a mattress that might as well have been a concrete block for all the forgiveness it graced on my back. The two cats Jude and Francie were so stressed out by the intruders that one fell ill and spotted the entire house with a bleeding and pissing urinary tract infection. New furniture and fabrics were being bartered over in China, and would be shipped over next week. My roof was being re-shingled. The floorboards in the main dining room were replaced by "real wood" which probably meant wood from a nearly extinct tree that had been genetically engineered by Buddhist scientists, sung to in the morning and peed on at night to ensure optimum health for the tree and good luck for me. My first night back I chose to sleep on the chair in my office, sitting up straight enough for an interview, and all of a sudden very loathe to remove the make-shift hat that nicely draped over my itchy, suffocating head and growing beard.

CHAPTER 11

In sleep he sang to me, in dreams he came. That voice which calls to me, and speaks my name. And do I dream again, for now I find, the PHA—NTOM OF THE OPERA is here, inside my mind. I pushed and pulled and kicked myself around my colorless, scentless, tasteless underground river of an office in my wheeled ergonomic gondola, singing like a half-faced madman, sporting a hunchback, looking for my lost slipper, knocking papers and trays off of my tables and desks, until my breathing became heavy and I fell back asleep.

CHAPTER 12

I navigated the house in the early hours before the warmth of day had woken anyone else up, making sure that, well, I'm not sure of the purpose of my dazed perambulation. I emotionally pawed at many of the familiar gold-leaf frames and gourd-like lamps and found German-legged chairs just where I'd expect them to be. I also tripped over a cardboard box near my dining room and got tangled in the wires of a portable lamp that was clipped to a door frame in bad taste. Once, I touched a head of hair that turned out to be a cat, maybe sick little Francie, quickly leaping out of reach. The familiarity, not just of shapes, distances, and angles, but also of intangibles such as the small wind that dripped in from the kitchen to the bar area carrying the smell of old wood and the sound of itself; the buoyancy of carpet on the stairs versus the woven rugs near the fireplace, how they felt like two completely different universes in my fingers; watching these details assault me from the other side of this gunny sack was a little comforting. Once, I giggled out loud. I stood at my window that overlooked Andom Bay, and, seeing nothing, cried for a half second, pressing my warm palms up against the cool glass. Transferring emotion. Spanning time.

The day was long in starting. I was hesitating unnecessarily like a kid in the school play, like a lamb before the slaughter, like the cough before consumption. When I hesitate, I repeat variations on a theme over and over in my head in order to prevent the next thought from coming along. I put a quick end to the encroaching madness of paralysis, returned to my office, and searched for the mask remover and eye patch which, it turns out, were knocked under the desk, finally found only when I heard chuckling behind the door and let Simon and my three sisters in to help the pathetic blind man out.

They rolled me out in my chair and, through a series of verbal hints and suppressed cackling, I quickly discovered that the hour was not as early as I had presumed, that it was merely a cold day at noon, and my misguided wanderings about the house had been silently observed by all members of my family, as well as Benedict Simon. They had watched me silently from quiet couches, moving their heads like frightened cats when touched. I called Astrid on a disposable phone I had previously slipped into my pocket, and asked her to meet me at my house at her earliest convenience. Seconds later she slinked down the stairs, the creaking gave her away, slowly as if feigning shame for having been present during the festivities and taking no protective action on my behalf. My presence would not be diminished so easily, and I asked her to grab the camera out of my pocket and document the unveiling of my head in fourteen million megapixels. I called Daniel quickly and asked him if he would be interested in covering the uncovering of my grand tête. I called the Mumford sisters, Annabelle and Zoë, and asked them if they were free for lunch, hell come over right now and we'll embark after the event. A few more phone calls later and the city was in an uproar responding to my quiet and desperate plea for attention and validation. My parents loved it, of course, in their one thousand years old but never tired way, for they invented media bending. My childhood had shotgun blasts of news crews during family fights, cold nights on the pristine city streets waiting for the emergency broadcast of our house burning down, interviewing the victims of meaningless lay-offs at my father's real estate company (those down-to-earth stories being the chief motivation for the layoffs in the first place). A city without news was not a Top Ten city, end of story. Now, even though my father would like to see nothing more than for Andom Bay to get bought out by Willchester and dragged through Victor and Jack's filth, the bounce in his laugh brought me back to an alternate universe where I wanted nothing more than that laugh to be directed towards something I had done. It had only taken eighty-nine goddamned years.

508 Incomplete Street was equipped with a long media driveway and parking lot for just this type of occasion. The crew from each channel could pull up their van, set up their signal, and position their talent in orderly rows and in such a way as to display the most favorable side of the house that swept up the aluminum façade and rolled over to a view of the city behind. My house staff dragged out the portable living room studio onto the side yard so that we could re-enact all of the proceedings without crowding into or dirtying up the actual room in question. Not knowing what the crews would want, and in which order, I asked Director of House Staffing and Support Sally to set up the

office studio and the bathroom studio in the back, just in case. I coached the teleprompters to pitch the story like this.

Founder and CEO of The Andom Bay Company and Chance Industries Anselm Betty returns home today after a one week stint in dumpy Gray Memorial, and we join him here to follow the story of his swift and miraculous recovery as family, friends, and loved ones from around the globe gather to support him. Taking a quick glance around, we see many people you the viewer may be familiar with, it's really quite astounding the circle of friends that Mr. Betty has, including, but certainly not limited to, his renowned mother and father Earl and Nancy Betty, acclaimed entrepreneurs and local celebrities Victor and Jack Grey, the Mumford sisters whom you may recognize from perfume commercials and the hit band Inconsistent, the owner of many of your favorite local restaurants Kenneth Mealy, Anselm's good friend and business partner Simon Meany, and the list just goes on and on. On the plate for this afternoon's event we will have the long-awaited *unwrapping* of Mr. Betty's head for the first time since its brutal and inexplicable stabbing just seven days ago.

They joined me now as I took my seat on the marble stool carved in the shape of Krishna's head and told them where they could stand. This bag had, in the course of the week, cast a new permanent symbol not only onto but also into my head as if I was now permitted to permanently lay claim to the whole family of blindness metaphors, eye similes, Cyclops references, and scarecrow analogies. Bag as metaphor for senselessness. Bag as cocoon. It was a glorious new world I would be emerging into, saturated with luxurious references to myself. What more could one ask for other than a gift certificate to the cryogenic graveyard?

I fired off the interviews one-by-one, just as self-indulgently and predictably as one would expect, with a few notable exceptions. One station, choosing to forsake the head unwrapping angle, brought up instead the family angle, looking for a retrospective of powerful family influence both in Willchester and Andom Bay. I took the opportunity to outline the events quickly since, as often as it had been told, all good histories need to be repeated, reiterated, and refreshed often and enthusiastically. Even then, perhaps only 60% of the citizens knew the story well enough to tell it themselves. If we were granting wishes today, you would be telling me that this number was nearer to 90%. True knowledge penetration was a myth, but one I fancied so well that I chose to become obsessed by its dangling carrot of a hope. The Manfred Betty clan pulled several families up the coast initially. The Goods were a competing lumber family; the Diedrichs and the Shins, rich and bored family friends, brought the arts and politics; the Gray family were nothing more than primitive gold diggers and desperate entrepreneurs, and they came uninvited. Of course, there were thousands of other families that came up during the following decades, but they came up because of these first families. These first few families begame powerful city nodes, settled in, and built up independent satellite corporations to keep themselves busy while their true businesses remained rooted in other cities in other parts of the world. They gave the rest of the population jobs. Eventually the satellites grew and gained satellites of their own. Over the next century certain Willchester city blocks were marked out by the interaction of emergent laws to be neighborhoods for the rich, neighborhoods for the poor, the restaurant and club district, the market and the parks. A baby growing arms and legs with no head in site. The Diedrichs put forth significant effort to improving the city by randomly supporting the businesses of friends—from clothing outlets to public schools to fruit stands and auto repair shops. The Shins focused exclusively on newspapers, then, when they came, radio and television. The Betty clan abandoned lumber and began to quietly accumulate land and real estate until they owned a majority of the business and residential space in the city. And the Greys controlled them all by infiltrating the political circles and gaining a few key players during critical times. Unscrupulous and shrewd, they amassed power and kept it by bullying richer, more powerful families around with hubris alone.

When I came onto this complicated board game in my early twenties, there was that short stint working for the Greys whereupon I became disillusioned and motivated enough to create an alternative to their "One City" one-sided propaganda. Andom Bay was formed and grew very successful very quickly, largely attributable to the voluntary relocation of the Shins, the Goods, and the Diedrichs. The total creative and financial support of these families now powering a new, more modern, city, led to a mostly-friendly sibling rivalry between the two cities. One old, organic, and sprawling, the other new, intentionally designed, and compact. These four most influential families continue to participate in the building of our beautiful city even now, as they all have representatives in the Board of Directors, and several prominent businesses; they have also spawned a colorful and oftentimes melodramatic cast of dysfunctional, spoiled, mad, and genius characters. However, on occasions like today, it's great to see that the rivalry falls to the wayside when confronted with the even more grand themes of origin, family, and friends. Still, I would not be surprised if there were one or two unexpected events that came about as a result of the volatile mix of personalities we have here today.

Channel 6 had the pleasure of covering a number of those unexpected events. Simon, I heard reported, had a small demonstration of Study Boxes set up gathering information on the news crews themselves. The boxes were configured to record density of people within several ten-foot by ten-foot areas. Victor and Jack Gray were putting several of them to stress and environmental tests to see how they would weather being doused in wine, or being kicked around like a soccer ball. My father called one interviewer a coconut. A press tent collapsed with my mother inside.

I was eager to delay the unwrapping for as long as was possible given the attention span of competing news crews. The longer they stayed, the more obvious it should become to Simon that this city was not done with me, that I could ride the wave of this bandaged head even with a bandaged head. The man who would emerge in perhaps less than ten television minutes would not be someone simple to destroy, not someone who would lay down and die, especially if power, politics, and persuasion were involved, for I had been throwing this party from long before he was even born. As soon as I could see his face, I would remove his smug ugly grin.

CHAPTER 13

I'm not a vain man, I don't bully others around because of deep unresolved issues regarding low self-esteem. I'm simply seeking the traditional and zen-like blurring between myself and my environment. I am in constant pursuit of a state where my will could flow seamlessly from my network of neurons to the larger network of buildings, people, hills, and lives around me. Chance was my vehicle, my flight from zero to infinity that stops off in Mr. Roboto land. At final baggage claim I would pick up the cancellation of the body and the self. I had man-like enemies, but you should consider the real enemy to be the world. Interpret men like Simon as inanimate objects that exert pressure against my identity as it dissolved into the world. To bring back the Agent and Landscape metaphors, it was a trick of the game to realize that the Agent didn't need to disappear in order for the Agent to become the Landscape, the man to become the world, for they were never separate in the first place. In fact, the Agent must remain defined and central to the Landscape at all times, as a, for lack of a better term, decoy. A beacon that pulled the watcher's eye forward and distracted him while the Landscape came in and strangled him.

And who, you might ask, was the royal He? Nobody but the Agent, the Landscape, the man, and the world himself. I've lost control of my vehicle and have spun out on the pavement many a time due to that bump. This was not the manifesto of an atheist. I was merely stating that the system we were given at birth was self-contained, all walls and no way out, but it didn't solve several paradoxes such as who made the system, who built the walls. I took the event of Creation on faith because logic, no matter how complex, couldn't explain how something came from nothing and this impossible event, however it happened, would take the most Inconsistent, Illogical, Paradoxical, Supernatural,

Unpredictable Being never to have been invented but who was Just Always There. I worshipped this God as I did the ties on my rack, the wings on my boots, and the curls in my coif: passionately, indifferently, completely, absent-mindedly.

I was gossiping with the Talent, turning the cameras away from this and towards that, encouraging directions for interviewers to take when talking with my parents, my friends, and Simon. I knew the viewers would not allow much more of a delay and at precisely that point I had one of my sisters yank the cur-tain back to reveal the gilded full body mirror that would tell me when the time came whether or not I was the most beautiful man in the world. Net-works broke to commercial and promised to cover the unwrapping when they returned. I took my seat, and asked Astrid to begin taking her pictures. I felt my face through the layers of tape, bandage, plaster, and cloth as if calming down a wild dog, or an ill rabbit. My face flinched and pulsed under its cage. Which Esmerelda or Christine would love this face when it was revealed? No, I did not ask for that kind of love—a woman who looked past exteriors and loved the man within (assuming even that was worth the effort) must have either been broken in such a tragic and horrible manner to have unlearned such powerful and ingrained laws of society, and one must assume that many other more useful laws of society could have easily been shattered in that same swipe, or she must be too dull or backwards to have learned them in the first place. No, the hypothetical woman who loved me, and whom I could love in return, was a mathematical impossibility, an imaginary number, for either I would be too ugly and evil for her sophisticated nature or she would be too broken and isolated for a superficial and shallow man like me. Let's take this off.

I picked at a piece of tape at the base of my neck, and peeled it up and around my shoulder. I held three long strips out with my right hand and some-one took them away. The set was chill and quiet. I straightened my collar, fin-gers fumbling on the fabric. I heard the click and whirr of mechanical gears, and felt myself passing out. I bit my tongue and hoped the nerves would carry outward with the pain a message to stay awake. Must breathe shallowly and evenly. Keep the head clear. Remain human.

So I told a story. A simple one that anyone could understand. It was about a man, an acquaintance of mine, Mr. Whitman Nordstrom, who everyone thought was a little bit eccentric. He was a folk musician, a street musician, and he wrote songs about the people he knew, which happened to be the people in my neighborhood here in Andom Bay. He probably wrote ten original songs a day; he was very prolific. As I walked to the train every morning he would test a new song on me. This is a simple story, don't expect too much from it, I'm not even entirely sure why I'm telling it now, but please just bear with me. Whitman was what most people would label as eccentric, like I said, and so he would sometimes take to pissing on cars in the streets as they drove by, or buying One Thousand Grand candy bars with the little money he made and hand them out to businessmen that walked by. He would sleep on the streets despite being the son of a wealthy family, one that I believe loved him very much and would never have turned him away if he ever came to them for help, which I don't think he did. He would never stay interested in a conversation long enough to complete it, even with his closest friends, but most people enjoyed his songs when they heard them. They were simple, ordinary songs, each one very similar to the next, but they were dependable and friendly. Occasionally, though I have to admit very rarely, insightful. I guess that's the story. Not really a story, is it? You might have expected someone to have ridiculed him publicly, or physically abused him, or that he got kicked out of town for sleeping on the streets, but to my knowledge none of that ever happened. Whitman Nordstrom.

I guess I was just thinking about him because I found out a week ago that he had died. Or rather, had drowned in the bay, while using a canoe. He frequently used the canoe to paddle from one side of the city to the other, perhaps to gain the benefit of different audiences at different times, Spanish guitar in tote. I read an article in the paper about it, maybe someone here wrote that article. The article was kind enough to say that it was an accident, though I'm not so sure it was. Not that it really matters now. Anyway, as far as I know, Whitman wasn't depressed, wasn't lacking friends, and may not have ever really been alone. In many respects, a full and ordinary life, with some quirks. That's all I was asking for, a full and ordinary life with some quirks. You'll know I'm done when you find me face down in Andom Bay, no sooner, no later. Until then, consider me in for the hand. And I'd like to think that there was a city that made that a possibility for others as well. Not that I want you all to drown yourselves in the bay, not at all, if you think that then you've missed the point of this story. I know, not very well told, but oh well, where were we?

I lifted the bag off my head, revealing a cast and bandages and more tape. Wind, cold wind, rushed up my red exposed nostrils. My mouth dried right up like a corpse. I could be such a cheese ball sometimes, it killed me. Carry on, carry on.

I felt around the cast, but couldn't find a handle or button or latch to pull on. Simon, can you grab the doctor, I think this next layer will need to be cut. Starting from the back of my neck, I felt the pressure of scissors on plaster and bandages clamp down and separate thick material. As he worked his way up my skull, I felt my head opening up, a great pressure being released. The doctor was very gentle with the operation, and soon the cold scissor navigated clear of my damaged eye and curved around my nose. The scissor departed and two gigantic hands lifted the cast off of my skull like two halves of a coconut chopped open with an axe.

Emergence. Coldness. Panic. I covered my face with my hands, feeling more bandages, more tape, all concentrated around my eyes in particular. The top of my scalp was now exposed and I presume the audience was greeted with a bed of unwashed and thinning hair flapping and twisting like vines off my head. Fantastic. Now, directing my fingers on the lock around my eyes as if I were a man pushed overboard in a straitjacket, I could sense for the first time the visual cues of movement. Dark to light, light to dark: a binary sort of vision. Zeros and ones drifted by, perhaps an emergency message in Morse code. I got it open, and lifted the crown of scabbed up tape and thorns off my head and started pulling the stray wisps of hair into the closest semblance of order possible (those that didn't fall directly out at first touch). Voices immediately lit up and began reporting events over the wire, broadcasting the first images available of the decrepit Mr. Betty, masochist and billionaire, comedian and dictator. The face made available in the mirror in front of me was outlined by the bridge of my nose, overarching brow, and gaunt cheek, a face considerably aged, pale, sunken, tired, unsymmetrical, and yet, somehow, unnaturally aware of its surroundings like an intelligent and dying beast from the dinosaur age. A wooly mammoth encased in ice.

The gilded frame of the mirror was packed with stainless steel knives of all sizes pointing in all directions. Every reflection of metal was a violation on my remaining eye, a knife pointed directly at me, one which I could not tell the distance, speed, or intention of. The faces of people around me were exaggerated moons of fake flesh, shiny with sweat and hazy with imagined cigar smoke. And flat flat flat, all of it flat.

CHAPTER 14

I was old, I had aged. I am an old man. While in the box with Schrödinger's cat I was neither here nor there, neither old nor young, but here I was, forced into a final state by observation itself since the law said I could not continue to be all things at once. Definition was a terrible thing, I much more preferred the purgatory of all possibilities to this, this terrible and frightened face.

The right eye had collapsed into itself, along with most of that side of my face. I've read about the right and left brain, how the right eye goes primarily to the left lobe and the left eye goes primarily to the right lobe, but would not be fooled into thinking that the left side of my brain was now without sight. I remember too the conflicting high school lesson that taught us that each eye was equipped with wires that led to the control panels of both lobes. I would turn into neither the illogical artist nor the unimaginative counter of jellybeans in a jar. Rest you assured. Worry not.

The Mumford sisters stood at the windowed door to my study, one in front of the other in overlapping pastels, dangling my eye patch tauntingly in front of me like the multi-armed goddesses of some professional corporate-sponsored religion. I indicated the knob for they were capable adults and could help themselves.

Annabelle and Zoë, the love of my life (singular), stepped into the office and Zoë helped attach the pirate's patch on my collapsed balloon of a face. The sisters were not complements of one another, nor were they foils—they were completely separate from one another. The traits of one were non-transferable to the other, nor did their traits follow any patterns of association to their personalities so that one might be able to make educated guesses about them and their individual preferences based on some general rule. Annabelle worked in commercials at Una Shin's Handsome Advertising, she was primarily a stand in or background presence, as she was not particularly striking by herself. Her beauty worked best when supplementing others. Zoë was the keyboardist in a local band, Inconsistent, and occasionally sang back-up vocals. I had courted them both, individually, a couple decades ago, but had never been able to decide which of the two sisters I loved more. It was as if, rolling ten die, two consecutive rolls both added up to a solid fifty-five each time, but each roll had a different set of numbers on different die that added up to that number. The rolls were of equal value, but their configurations were different. After years of frustration which I've both idolized and repressed into the depths of my deepest memory, they grew tired of the game and both eventually married less perfect matches, and have since built successful and happy families around that move. Far from driving us apart, this brought us closer together (since the primary stale mate had been erased from the board out of respect to society's rules) and has allowed me to move the question offline where I've secretly continued playing, every day trying to decide which sister I loved more, which one I loved more completely, with no doubt. A question of such weight can never be answered arbitrarily or by random draw, as that would deflate all weight in the answer. And in this state I've been paralyzed for over twenty years, unable to force my will to choose between two perfect and equal beings, even long after the answer would have led to a legal move.

We bantered about recent events, I cajoled them about their blatant self-promotion for daring to show up at such an event, Annabelle jabbed me about my choice of Eastern Religion stool, and Zoë said she wanted to fall face down into her glass of Merlot during my story about Whitman and scolded me for not giving her band a chance to play a soundtrack to my miserable event. Flirting with them was as dull and refreshing as it ever was, and soon I was showing Zoë pictures from my digital camera that were taken mere minutes after leaving them at the Yellow Monkey, and confiding in Annabelle about Simon's ghostly hand in the whole matter.

CHAPTER 15

With eye-patch and bowling hat, my presence became significantly less horrifying. I showed the girls my new (to them) shoes, the Salvatore Ferragamos, the very ones I had tap danced down the halls of Grey Memorial in, and Zoë showed me her new turquoise Frye Daisy Dukes that she had purchased off of the Internet. Annabelle straightened my hat and kissed my cheek, relating to me the tale of the horrible shoes she had to wear in Cindy Rickblank's campaign short film. I love uncomfortable shoes—I'm a completely impractical man in that regard—I love the tight, misshapen shells that restrict and pinch my swollen toes as I hobble down the cobblestone driveway of my home to the center of all Andom Bay life. Their tension provides a confining context within which the rest of my body can stand secure and sure of itself.

Annabelle and Zoë pardoned my unsure steps and slow meandering shuffle that was my walk and agreed to accompany me on a tour through the city. I was supposed to take walks, see people, and interact, but I wasn't very fast. I wasn't fast in general, with anything, really. It didn't take too great of a literary critic to determine what happened in stories where characters lived fast and died young. I've read to the end of the story many a time, stories that have begun and ended within my larger story. I moved in slow motion, I let the shot clock run to the absolute end before shooting. When a house was built directly in the line of sight between my balcony and Green Light Park, I typically waited until the entire building was completed, the tenants had moved in, and they'd all switched their mailing addresses and checkbooks over, before passing a new law that required its immediate demolition. The delayed period of time between the act that upset me, and my response (move and countermove), had gone a long way in contributing to my current troubles as it created an ominous cloud over every action by another, not knowing whether or not I approved of anything until much later. It seemed to have turned Simon against me. The intimidation factor was the evil taint that corroded me and all business men like me. It was like a certain ring in a certain book, essential for success, but in the end it corrupted and corroded even the most innocent and ethical minds. Luckily, I've read these books too and know how they end. I try to keep my heart untethered from the dark side, I really do. Just take a look at these light feet kicking down the street right now, are they evil?

Annabelle said, "Simon doesn't have the history that you do. His name doesn't begin with paddling up the coast in the 18th century and end with Betty."

My fortune cookie once read: formulas for success are many. Simon may not have the name but he had the distributed network of influence in Chance 1.0, and eventually Chance 2.0, to compensate for anything he lacks in namesake etymology. I would say that at this point we were equal opponents, just as Victor and Jack had been for me up until now. In all honesty, I preferred it this way, when the opponent was equal the soul springs to life. The game was fair, and all bets are even. It was the magic mixture of tension and weight that brought out the best in us all. Bring it on! Cheerleader kick.

Zoë said, "This corner of Incomplete and 1st would be perfect for my band to play on. Can we zip quickly into this café and ask? What's this?"

A crowd was gathered around a large steel video billboard, ten feet tall, five feet wide, one large screen occupying the majority of the surface and a smaller screen directly above it, cement still drying and yellow plastic tape around the immediate vicinity to prevent people from getting too close. On the large screen was a solid orange background and the words "Handsome Advertising Presents. Relevant Billboards. Local Participating Businesses Include. Café Quine. Andom Bay Food Market Store. Starbucks. AMC 7th Ave Theaters. More Coming Soon. For More Information. Contact Handsome Advertising. 415-2685." The screen went blank, then the orange background came on again and repeated its message. Entering the café, Anthony Dumont was pulling a table out from the back and wiping it off simultaneously. A carafe of warm coffee and a bowl of oranges arrived in his steady hands a few seconds later and he pulled out the chairs for the ladies and we sat down for a chat. Anything for Mr. Betty and his friends. He congratulated Annabelle on her stunning appearance in Cindy Rickblank's short film, she played a stunning damsel in distress. The film was playing on the new Relevant Billboard near the Good Library and City Hall. Anthony had bought the standard package first thing this morning and could not wait to see his commercial pop up all over the city according to the algorithm. Brilliant concept, Mr. Betty, perfectly brilliant. He excused himself when two other customers indicated their need for a bill.

One carafe of coffee later Zoë acquired her gig, and I called Astrid to make sure that Café Quine's advertising budget was supplemented with a 100% matching donation from us. Our next stop, the Good Library, did not go as smoothly. The librarian, Thomas Seller, had not noticed our arrival and we discovered the shelves to be rather disorderly and the air conditioning to be on too strongly. I was appalled to see that they had not yet connected their inventory databases up with Chance's network, rendering it impossible for anyone but the library staff to know which books were available without physically stepping into the building themselves. In fifteen minutes I had some technicians from Chance Industries and neighborhood managers from the Andom Bay Company at the location, installing new hardware and hooking them up to the network. Zoë tugged on my sleeve and pulled us out to the sidewalk, Annabelle carried in her arms three new releases that she had checked out.

"You need to forget about work, Anselm, it will only stress you out," said Zoë. "That should be reserved for the neighborhood managers at The Andom Bay Company, not the CEO."

My heart was beating unevenly and lopsidedly. I realized then that this city would atrophy into so many unconnected particles of dream dust the minute I was no longer driving it. I had only been OOTO for a week and already management was getting lazy and workers were taking short cuts. I would take the next train to Willchester, and set things again into neat and orderly rows. Everything would be ducky again.

I did not take the next train though, at least not the one going east. Annabelle convinced me that I had time to spare, that I should instead spend the rest of the afternoon with her, for we had not had the chance to in so long. Zoë and I agreed to visit our experimental sub-city named Little Anhedonia, a short thirty-minute train ride outside of Andom Bay, to the west.

Little Anhedonia was to Andom Bay as Andom Bay was to Willchester: an even smaller, more perfect, more progressive, more designed, less real, less depressing, less futile; a city within a city, a company within a company. I started Little Anhedonia five years ago as a 401K of sorts, as a place I planned to retire to eventually. The Board of Directors had grown large in Andom Bay and some had grown tired of the increasing bureaucracy and decided to break off into a sub-board that gained jurisdiction over a small piece of land outside of town, and could co-exist within the larger structure while still having its own independence. Every one of the thousand or so citizens of Little Anhe-donia was a full-time employee of The Anhedonia Company, a subsidiary of the Andom Bay Company, basically a tax write-off for us. Their job: to enact the roles they might otherwise play in a real city, and through acting, find meaning in the role. There were twenty or so people who were hired to pretend to work at the Anhedonia Company (even though they, and everyone else in the city, actually did), and they had their offices in Andom Bay for the same reason we in the Andom Bay had our offices in Willchester. The rest of the population woke up at their normal times in Little Anhedonia, went to their normal jobs, lived their normal lives, and the setup served superbly as a tourist spot and curiosity for most people outside of it. In Little Anhedonia, I was Mayor.

We pulled into the only train station around 4:30pm and the jolly conductor winked at me as he helped me off the platform. Zoë loved this town, and constantly asked people what their jobs were, what their families were like, and what the kids wanted to be when they grew up. Annabelle treated everyone in Little Anhedonia as she would in Andom Bay, with a cold shoulder.

Zoë asked the conductor, "Where do you go for your vacations, conductor?"

"Willchester, of course."

We had dinner at the Blue Kangaroo, the town's hot spot for celebrities and wannabe hipsters alike. Previously, I had gone to my Anhedonia hotel room number 9876 and changed into my favorite periwinkle suit and black shirt for the night. Always black. The paparazzi were there, snapping pictures of us for tomorrow's copy, which we posed seductively for.

Annabelle said, "Tomorrow let's you and I go have lunch with Simon. Maybe this mix-up has all been due to a little communication breakdown, and a light talk over some red wine and a dozen cheeses will clear it right up."

I did not want to talk about Simon anymore. He was a good man, but sometimes two good men could disagree, couldn't they?

"In this case, you two disagree over the fact of whether you should be alive or dead, but fundamentally it's the same as any other disagreement, and as such should be resolved with a clear presentation of the facts: a business case, and a solid investigation of return on investment."

We used net present worth now. NPW.

"Whatever."

Zoë liked red wine in Andom Bay, but drank exclusively white wine here. She also never wore her wedding ring in Little Anhedonia. We chatted about a new idea I had had while in a coma. The assumptions in the coma were as follows: Simon had a network of one hundred thousand computers in Andom Bay, all of which were connected to local businesses, parks, street corners, signal lights, elevators, cafés, libraries, and now Relevant Billboards. That network was built in such a way as to provide a hierarchy of data that was available to different users who had different privileges on the system. There was currently a way to write queries on the data, assuming you had appropriate privileges, however it required that you have an intimate knowledge of the structure of the data, which was not ideal and made the practicality of such an interface almost null. The final product was a vast collection of disparate data that was all machine-readable, aggregatable, and consumable, but only by experts. What was missing was a human interface, a way to directly communicate with Chance from any one of its nodes around the city. That's what this Golden Box that I dreamt about was, an API into Chance which allowed communication through a simple scripting language that was composed of human-producible sounds rather than text. The human scripting language, named GoldenScript in my dream, would be based on the simple rules of Propositional Calculus (I felt like I could write the grammar right now on this napkin!), and it was the killer app which Chance Industries had been waiting for and which could motivate the company into 2.0, 3.0, and beyond. Not until Zoë nodded her head slowly, and licked the seasoned fry seasoning off my pudgy fingers, did I realize that I had had my first grand vision since the previous one (Andom Bay itself).

Most of the patrons in the Blue Kangaroo pretended to enjoy their meals, since it was their job, but I had to admit that I was not so pleased with mine. As Mayor I exercised my mayoral right to fire the cook (from the restaurant, not the Anhedonia Company), and forced the restaurant to find a new cook who actually knew what they were doing in the kitchen. Because I knew the previous cook was not a bad man, I offered him a job at the Anhedonia Law Offices as a district judge if he promised to let me have an appointment with him early the next morning.

Independently of one another, Annabelle and Zoë had announced to the courtroom at large the existence of two critical new elements of evidence that would be relevant to the case of Betty vs. Andom Bay: one, a new project (GoldenScript) which would propel Anselm's will into the furthest corners of Andom Bay, and two, a business case that supplemented GoldenScript, one that simply stated that it was most profitable for both the defendant and the prosecutor if I remained in existence. This new evidence, consisting of two documents, had come to me so conceptually complete (for I could even see their cover letters, the type of paper they were printed on, and in what size font) that it was utterly inconceivable to me that they had not yet been created. Simpler to think that they had been downloaded directly to me, in whole, perhaps printed on dream paper, and that I merely inherited the task of translating them into this world's language. Like On The Road. Like Frankenstein. Like the Holy Bible. I would give birth to these documents of salvation myself, and it would be easy, and it could not wait.

I invited the two sisters to stay with me in Little Anhedonia, and offered to call their husbands and children to ask permission.

"My children are all grown up, Anselm."

My motives were not completely noble. I implied though trained facial expressions and a delayed cadence in my voice my old-man-on-the-verge-of-mental-breakdown persona. The story of an Anselm who wished to take a short vacation with close friends. Of course, it was just as much a story of an old man stalling as he chose between the two women he loved. I was both of these contradicting people at once, and even though on paper it looked wrong, immoral, my conscience throughout was white as snow, white as snow. Pinning down motivations to actions was always an imprecise and misleading tail-to-donkey business, as we had to assume for simplicity's sake that the mind was merely digital, that it was a collection of a limited set of on/off switches that could only be activated one at a time. Whereas I found that my own motivations were often Rubik's Cubes of intertwining, conflicting reasons, which I could arrange to look simple and complete, or twist a few times and represent as utter disorganization and chaos, something untranslatable into words. Whether or not I was good or evil was a function of the tools which were processing this complex information and translating it into one or the other—in the end, it was just a matter of whether or not the machine rounded up or down. To make matters less clear, Annabelle and Zoë both claimed to have already called and purchased enough leave from their families to see me through.

I called Astrid to give her my instructions for tomorrow. Send a notary, my laptop, my two tan filing cabinets, and a case of my Krug 1988 Vintage Brut. She said that a delivery matching those exact specifications (plus envelopes and postage, which I realized I had forgotten about) was sent on the eight o'clock express and, as if on cue, I saw a blinking light on my hotel phone possibly informing me of their delivery downstairs. She reported in other news that Simon had revealed a new Study Box test at today's late afternoon senior management team meeting. It involved a new microscopic Study Box prototype that could be manufactured so cheaply that it was cost-effective to distribute them in vaporous clouds in the hopes that a few of them might find their way somewhere that would provide useful information. They were small enough to be inhaled, at which point they would attach to the lining of your lungs, harmlessly one hoped, and transmit an encrypted unique identifier out via radio waves. If these tiny Study Boxes were within fifty feet of other Study Boxes like them, they would also pass on the transmissions of other boxes, so that hopefully the majority of the signals would return to Chance. Same basic idea of the larger Study Boxes, but their portability and easy distribution gave them an extra insidious power. Using triangulation data obtained by the paths of each signal's transmission, their locations would then be mapped onto a larger grid and display the distribution of infected people as they went about their daily business. He had tested it out at the media event for the unwrapping of my head, and had since whittled down the set of all unique identifiers to include only those that had moved outside of the original radius of the cloud within the first few hours. This meant deleting the data from 99% of the Study Boxes that had fallen onto the marble tile of my faux living room, missing the gaping mouths of spectators. The preliminary data, Simon said, had promise. Simon's plan was to map the traffic patterns of this test group to see if it could be statistically correlated to any other data set that had been gathered about the city using other means. If successful, technology like this could be sold to businesses so that they could know roughly where their customers were at any given time, and thus provide more targeted marketing and more effective incentives to its customers. This new product fell under the jurisdiction of the recently passed law that allowed aggregation and selling of customer information when individual identity was not compromised. Even before I went to bed, I knew that this one was going to haunt my dreams.

Annabelle rented the room one door east of me, and Zoë took the room to the west.

CHAPTER 16

I rose early and got dressed before the sisters were expected to wake up. From the neck down I was a stunning model of a successful entrepreneur, as convincing and indestructible as I have ever felt. I was embarking again into that imaginary world of the mind where I would hunt and kill the object of my thoughts and drag it into the startling light of day where all could see. The single most satisfying thing I've ever done. The two rows of silver buttons on my suit jacket glimmered like the keys of a xylophone, playing my superhero theme song with reflected light. The morning fog had rolled into the hotel's lobby, casting a tomb-like haze over the wooden crates that stood by the elevator, the contents of which were half a century of notes, each note unconnected to the rest, spanning topics as incongruent as poker tricks and system administration and cat health and gardening tips and ethical wartime philosophy and manifestoes for raising children; a database of thoughts indexed and referenced only by number, related to one another by no common element other than the hand with which they were written, and their ordering by ascending time.

I held my camera out at arm's length with both hands and snapped a picture of me as I spun in a circle, then slid it back into my pocket and stepped out onto the street. Perhaps I loved myself too much. I found myself to be too clever. One small breakthrough and all of a sudden I could do no wrong. I always grew quiet and suspicious whenever the signs of happiness exhibited too vividly. Stop smiling, Anselm, or you would ruin everything and it would all be your fault. The streets were quiet, although the first hints of commuters biking and walking and driving to work shaded the city. It was very convincing. I even saw a paper boy, knocking down mailboxes with the daily news. I wasn't paying them enough do deserve this faithfulness, this attention to detail. For a split second, I saw everything through a watery lens.

The new judge was removing plants from boxes into his new office when I knocked and entered. He thanked me again, and I bowed deeply in return, for I was about to ask him a big favor. We deliberated for a bit regarding the appropriate room within which to talk, and since he hadn't yet seen the court-room, we decided to visit that as we talked. All of Little Anhedonia's laws were confined to the city itself. In addition, they inherited all the laws of Andom Bay so that when the local laws were silent, those of the parent family were allowed to speak up. Finally, if there was a conflict between an Anhedonia law and an Andom Bay law, the Anhedonia law held precedence. My favor was this: I asked that the judge propose a local instance of the contract known as marriage, so that, within city limits, it was defined as a custom wherein two people agree to be life-time partners within, and only within, the city limits of Anhedonia. This would not conflict with the more conventional law of marriage because this one did not claim to hold the same scope as the first, it did not claim to be everlasting, nor universally binding. The judge, and this was where I realized that he would be a good judge, asked why I didn't simply propose this new law myself, as I was acting Mayor. The answer was simple, and one due to a simple protective measure in the current body of laws that were in practice in Little Anhedonia: only a judge could propose a new law out of turn, and I could not afford to wait for my turn. The new judge, certainly a quick thinker, then asked whether or not I was in fact going to ask someone to marry me soon. Alas, no, I had no such plans. He confessed to being confused, but was tactful enough to not press me further, and promised to do as I had asked.

I knelt at a rock on the way back home, catching my breath. The inhales brought in the turquoise sky and mustard yellow clouds, the exhales displayed a dimpled spider, fat and white, on a white heal-all holding up a moth like a white piece of rigid satin cloth. I knew what I was doing. When investing heavily in one sector of the market, invest equally as much in another, contra-dicting sector. Balance your eggs, hedge your bets. The documents I would begin typing up today would go a long way towards sealing my fate with regards to my role at Chance Industries and the Andom Bay Company. It was time to release control of another equally vital sector of my life by moving the control panel of love and marriage and eternal happiness out of my basket and into Annabelle's and Zoë's. I would not define the rules for them, nor let them know that such rules even existed, but on the off chance that one of them ever choose to ask me to marry her (despite already being married to another man, despite polygamy not being an option, despite the absolute absurdity of such a possibility), I had just taken steps to ensure that there was a little corner of the world that would allow such a thing to blossom. And he lived happily, ever alone.

CHAPTER 17

I have not done justice to Annabelle and Zoë in my descriptions. Perhaps the emotions still swing too highly and wildly to capture and display without feeling like a lepidopterist. Hints of a romantic inclination tell me that I would be no better than a tourist who photographs and exploits his subjects in distant lands by putting their faces on cheap cardstock, than a Napoleon who chips the statues off of temples and carries them back to the Louvre, than a zookeeper who breeds white snow lions in captivity, to try to describe this focused ball of passion in my gut that spins and kicks for my constant attention. As long as you're interested in depraved lunatic souls who have transformed the beautiful and wild into polyester and porcelain merchandise, why don't you study these men as well? In any case, I will not let guilt paralyze me from lingering on trite phrases and inadequate descriptions. Many authors speak of a single vivid image that unfolds into an entire novel. They speak of a seed planted in their imaginative center that, for whatever reason, after a few cautious licks they have bitten into and have discovered an indescribable thing that resonated inside them like the single pitch of sound that can shatter a glass of wine. And it was that mysterious image which destroyed them so thoroughly that the novel fell out of their minds, whole.

Of the weeks that followed in Little Anhedonia, locked in our hotel, within which we wasted the lengthy ribbons of sunlight that the days had cut out for us under fluorescent bulbs, a single image stuck in my mind above the rest. I had installed a desk at the northern corner of my room which faced two curtained windows at right angles to one another, and through which I could just barely trace the arc of the winter sun through the thick canvas. Entire drawers of my filing cabinet had been displaced and dumped on the ground by my feet as I rooted through past records of test results, revenue statements for the two businesses, and press releases for long forgotten information. Using notepad, typewriter, laptop, and, when necessary, a permanent marker on the length of my forearm, I was drafting up first, second, third, fourth, fifth, and further drafts of my two documents, the GoldenScript Requirements Document and the Anselm Betty Business Case, and alternatively spinning left and right in my swivel chair, passing crumpled piles of shorthand off to either Annabelle or Zoë for proof-reading, editing, and personal opinions. I frequently begged them to leave, for they should be riding on the backs of camels and sleeping in canoes rather than slowly growing more and more pale in this chilled room with myself and my obsessions. At one point five or six days in, I spun left and handed the latest draft of the business case to Annabelle, then shortly afterward spun right and tossed the stapled manuscript of the GoldenScript document to Zoë, and realized that for the first time in a couple days I had no paper on my own desk to scribble on and rearrange text on. I turned fully around and focused my single eye on the light that reflected through it. There was a long red couch with short hand-carved wooden legs, round soft armrests, and dark gray diamonds interlaced throughout. On the left side of the couch sat Annabelle, her right elbow resting on the couch's arm and propping up her chin with her palm as she held the papers in her left hand and her hair covered her face. She was reclined on her side in a pastel blue summer dress with white stripes, and her legs folded out to her left with her knees bent and ankles crossed at the couch's center. Her toenails were painted white. Her elbows and knees were perfectly round. On the right side of the couch sat Zoë, a reflection of her sister's position, left hand dangling off the armrest, document in her right hand, legs folded to the right in long black slacks, wearing her hair up with a dozen barrettes, and a shawl covering her bare shoulders. I've told you about the short bouts of tears that can well up unpredictably on occasion, but this was night and day. If my heart were an engine, I had just slammed on the gas and the break simultaneously. Pulled concurrently to extreme motion and to perfect stillness, my heart just ceased to be for a few brief moments while I cried, laughed, hiccoughed and burped at the same time.

The heart returned and the world resumed and Annabelle and Zoë looked up from their papers at each corner of the couch. Sensing awkwardness approaching, Annabelle crossed her eyes and Zoë stuck out her tongue. They marked up my documents more harshly than normal that round, and I was busy revising and editing late into the night. Long after they returned to their rooms, I reflected once again on the moment during in the split second after work ended and before sleep came.

CHAPTER 18

I'm not entirely certain that Little Anhedonia even bothered to get up in the morning during those three introverted weeks. With no CEOs daring to venture forth into the town, there was no reason for them to wake up at 4am to deliver the pretend news to the pretend citizens, nor to open the cafés for their pretend customers prepared by their pretend cooks. In fact, I'm fairly certain that they all took the liberty of calling in sick and going to Willchester for a short vacation, pagers equipped with fresh batteries should their shy CEO ever decide to open that door to room 805 and walk out of the hotel. Thankfully, for them, he never did, and they were free to gyre and gimble in the wabe.

It's also a rhetorical question to debate about whether or not Andom Bay continued to exist, and while we're at it, even Willchester, during this time. Undoubtedly I have my own suspicions, but since there's no proof either way, I will reserve the voicing of opinions for more worthwhile debates. For example, the number of angels that can fit in the head of a pin. It's two. Two angels.

CHAPTER 19

The creative process that I embarked on appeared to mirror exactly one full cycle of destruction and creation. Life destroyed itself in order to bring new life into being, this way ensuring that our world never became more lively or orderly or creative than it had already been, just as it could not become more warm. You started with two tall tan filing cabinets, files organized chronologically, passionately self-referencing one another. You started with one freshly arranged hotel room, a desk in the corner, and a couch behind it. You started with a solved Rubik's Cube and three friends on vacation. The process kicked off and suddenly the drawers of the filing cabinet were removed and overturned. All order amongst files was erased as papers were first scattered all over the floors and then regrouped into new solar systems with Post-it Note moons: those pertaining to artificial intelligence, those pertaining to logic and calculus, those pertaining to linguistics, those pertaining to engineering, those pertaining to accounting and program management, those pertaining to mob theory, those pertaining to information theory. On top of these papers rested the trays and platters of obliterated entrees that were brought up to 805 by uniformed teenagers pretending to be room service attendants, and consumed by three friends who tossed around a Rubik's Cube that achieved increasing states of disorder. An informal one-pager that had originally been drafted for the timely completion of two documents was amended when it became clear that it would take more like four or five documents in order to do the job right.

What originally began as the Requirements Document for GoldenScript 1.0 was, after Zoë's brutal critique, put on hold until I had completed a Technical Specification that included a new hardware investigation. In addition to sheer hardware (perhaps a hundred new Golden Boxes, designed to specification), I would need to inject a couple new requirements into Simon's Chance 2.0 project (something I had been hoping to avoid but, alas, could not). Astrid faxed me the latest version of Simon's document which I revised and faxed back to her the next morning, attaching only the briefest of explanations, for Simon's sign-off. Simon took two days in getting back to me, but ultimately acquiesced to my request—which was a smart thing for him to do since I would've otherwise pulled out the two teams I had lent to him earlier this year. He needed those two extra teams in order to ensure that his maintenance and support team would meet their service level agreement contract that they had with The Andom Bay Company. He undoubtedly knew that. The Requirements Doc, Tech Spec, and Software Schedule for GoldenScript, despite it all, still came together a little ahead of plan, but unfortunately any time I gained there was lost when considered alongside the many days I spent spinning on the Business Case for continuing existence.

One of the major problems that I had not anticipated was the lack of data. I should've known better. I had not taken a single extended vacation from Chance Industries since it was founded over fifteen years ago. In fact, this was perhaps the first time ever that the company had gone more than a week without my charismatic presence. I've always believed that should I ever leave even for the briefest period of time, I would lose whatever advantage I had acquired over the forces of inertia and entropy. My business would inevitably make a single blind decision while I was gone and it would create a cascade of misaligned resources that eventually sapped the company of all life and energy. This mentality, which I was slowly falling away from, meant that I had no historical data to help approximate just how much my presence was worth to the company. Every project, every employee, every decision had been in some way touched by my influence, making it next to impossible to disentangle my value from my company's value. One might say that 100% of its value was due to me, but one could not guess how quickly that value would drop should my miniscule effect be removed from the system as a whole. Was I the glue, or the rot, on Chance Industries' wooden beams?

I turned instead to my second most valuable employee and estimated Simon's value by analyzing revenue statements during the years before he joined the company and those after. I cringed at the assumptions I was making (Was he really responsible for the decline in the Euro that year which allowed our zero-denominated debt to shrink, thus padding our revenue numbers? Could I really attribute the failures and successes of other projects in other departments to his influence? What about the earthquake that destroyed one of our remote data centers—must he take some of the blame for that?), and rounded every calculation down hoping that if I was ultra-conservative in my estimates perhaps that would sufficiently erase the chances that any one incorrect assumption would skew the final results too favorably. When I added up the numbers, Simon only had a ten-thousand dollar value his first year, and actually fell into the black his second year. His third year rang up to be over one hundred million (although one could argue that those savings came from the vast efficiencies of scale that the company had been edging towards long before he ever arrived), and last year he had once again cost the company something to the tune of twenty-five million. To draw a line through these numbers would be folly. If I were to take these numbers and say that I was somehow ten times more valuable that Simon to the company, I do not know if that would result in a gigantic number, or a negative one.

What if I counted the number of shares of publicly-traded stock I owned in the company and multiplied it by the current stock price? Was that my value to the company? Not precisely. I tried adding up the total number of extant shares and multiplying that by the current stock price. If I were to sell all of my shares, a majority 51% hold, how much would the stock price fall? Probably quite a bit, probably to zero. This was a good sign. If I triggered the selling of all of my shares on the public market to take place on the event of my death, it would be easy to assign a number to my value—again it approached 100% of the company's value. This would be sabotage though. Did I really want to link my immortality to my mortality in such a fatal way? Would it really be to my benefit to, upon leaving this world, also erase all trace of my existence by destroying that which I had built up? Afterlife or no, this world was real and would probably continue to be real long after I was gone. It was not a tough exercise of the imagination to see two alternative worlds after I was gone, one that included traces of me and one that did not, and knowing such, who would voluntarily choose the latter?

Annabelle said, "The stronger your business case is for continued existence, the weaker your posthumous legacy will be." Once articulated, the solution came to me quickly. My value would not be determined by assuming that the current business would lose value after my death, but rather that my worth was only as great as was my ability to create future incremental growth in the company's value during my remaining years. GoldenScript needed a business case of its own, and that would serve doubly as the business case for my future existence. I would simply have to stage the project in such a way that incremental revenue generated from the project was inextricably linked to my management of the project, and at no point could my presence become unessential. Chance Industries would live on either way, but the longer I lived with it, the better it would do after I was gone. After this breakthrough, the document was wrapped up fairly quickly (knowing now that it would not be anything but supplemental to my real business case) and I began work on the cornerstone document, GoldenScript's business case.

One hundred sleepless hours later, it was complete. I had five folders in my hands, all together containing approximately fifty-thousand words in double-spaced, 12pt Courier font. Elegant prose that, when considered together, presented a solid guaranteed that I would live at least another ten years. People would see to it. Should the Grimacing Reaper himself approach me now, I don't believe he would be able to deny the salient points made therein. The final day in Little Anhedonia was spent re-filing notes into my two tall tan filing cabinets, returning dishes to the kitchen, tossing out the old, empty, well-used bottles of Krug, and generally tidying up the room. In the morning, three enthusiastic men from the postage office hammered together another make-shift crate for the cabinets, and tilted it away. The only thing that would've been more aesthetically pleasing plot-wise would be if either Annabelle or Zoë had proposed. I do not know what they were thinking. They did not propose, and I only hesitated long enough to sigh heavily once while adjusting my collar, before we winked at the conductor and boarded the 7am train back to Andom Bay. We were three platonic friends sandwiched on a single bench facing the rear of the train, bumping along backwards as the landscape outside the window to our right scribbled words of reassurance in Mother Nature's soft malleable crayon. The sisters fell asleep on either side of me.

CHAPTER 20

Familiarity was a powerful foe, one that derailed progressive thought, numbed consciousness, swapped real objects for well-worn symbols, faulty representations, and closed off the mind from fresh or novel details. Train cabins became parodies of themselves. New revelations were viciously attacked by the nit-picking piranha of routine doubt. Did I really love Annabelle and Zoe? And thus the native hue of resolution is sicklied o'er with the pale cast of thought.

My seating position was uncomfortable, but fatally familiar. Every morning for as long as I could remember I had taken the train from the Andom Bay home to the Willchester offices sandwiched between two workers on their way to a construction site, or two ladies on their way to a book club, or a brother and sister on their way to a funeral, or two adulterers on their way back home from faux late nights at the office. Today it was Annabelle and Zoë, but perhaps that was a moot point, a curious detail for the historian or the detective, and people to remember should I ever need an alibi for something occurring precisely now, but certainly not important for the story at hand. I am a solitary man who keeps his hands to himself, tucked between his femininely crossed legs lest even his recently ironed sleeve make the slightest contact with the another passenger's clothing. Heaven forbid that flesh touch stranger flesh through a hundred layers of clothing anywhere except at the hip and at the shoulder, where it was absolutely necessary in these confined people spaces. Three weeks in Little Anhedonia and how long did my thoughts linger next to theirs? Did they ever enter my full attention for a single split second? Was my mind even spacious enough to permit the entrance of any thoughts other than my own, of any being other than myself, or was I all-consumed by my empty signifier, incapable of experiencing another being other than through the filters of my own fiction? Did you see the sisters with your own eyes? What mysterious and unnamed chamber did I presumably have prepared for the eventual love in my heart that wasn't long ago appropriated for the storage of my expansive library of self-sorrow? Our shoulders and hips pressed together in mock-urgency, but they were now both asleep, and anyway, did that make up for the thousands of miles of deserted wasteland between my heart and theirs? This was just the beginning of the self-destructive train of thought that I knew was now gaining speed and shuttling through each station of my over inflated self-confidence, twisting signposts, scraping the sides of buildings as it turned sharp corners, and admitting no new passengers of reason onto its mindless and never-ending journey. I had possibly wasted three valuable weeks of potential negotiation and intimidation instead writing poetry in a dark cave with two women, fooling myself into thinking that something could, or even should, happen. Must it be?

The low hum of the train hypnotized me with its steady rhythm of sounds that repeated every two seconds. Perhaps I was not fully awake, perhaps I too had fallen asleep on that suicidal trip. Perhaps I never uttered under my mocking and hateful breath, "I love you." A directionless, objectless, meaningless you that applied to everything I knew, hovering outside of space-time. My heart beat me up the rest of the way into town, and I thought perhaps I was having a heart attack.

CHAPTER 21

Instead of going directly to Willchester and delivering my manifesto to the Board immediately as planned, we disembarked wordlessly at Andom Bay and Annabelle held my hand and Zoë hooked her arm around mine and Annabelle placed her arm around Zoë's shoulder. We stood in a triangle on the empty platform at the edge of the empty station and cried, apologizing, wailing, drunk with sorrow. My eye-patch slid off and hooked itself around my nose. I am a ridiculous man. I don't remember how that particular day of my life ended, if it ever did.

CHAPTER 22

Damn. Damn post-modernism and the soul. Damn beauty and simplicity. Damn the reader, the writer, and the jolly ghost. God, if you can hear me, I believe, help my unbelief. Did my house really burn down? Fantastic! Did the newspapers really run that story about my adulterous vacation with the Mumford sisters? Fair play. Did Astrid really fall down the stairs and break her neck before the late firefighters could rescue her? Bloody figs.

CHAPTER 23

It was then that I began to make extensive use of the phrase, "Fine, thank you."
I spent more time thinking about my reaction than actually reacting, and
therefore lost any ability to mourn or even feel anything for a couple days at
least. I had become what my friends and critics had expected me to eventually
become: an emotionless man. There were some signs of my animal self rum-
bling deep below, sleeping or preparing an attack I could not tell, the one who
I'm told should've been angry, saddened, and exhausted all at once. They
sometimes call this thing the inner child, the inner man, though I think mine
had been neglected for so long and to such an extent that it did not deserve to
be called anything other than a rat, or a beetle, for it had lost all faculty of
thought and debate. Once though, during a distant burst of applause for which
I didn't know the source, my inner cockroach made me kick a plaster wall so
hard that I could feel my largest toenail fold into itself inside my shoe. It, the
nail, eventually fell off entirely, leaving a green and black scab in its place, and
months later a tiny newborn sliver of a toenail emerged, blinking its bewildered eyes at me. Another time I sat for an entire day in my Willchester office,
having run out of business cards but unable to bring myself to ask anyone
other than Astrid to order me new ones. Business cards had been a shared trial
between Astrid and I, although we had hated them for different reasons. She
was of the school that a business card should be informal and irreverent, a joke
of some sort or a conversation piece that you could pass around amongst
friends over cocktails and see who had the best one. I was much more serious
about them, unwilling to have an informal business card unless I myself was an
informal man. And yet, put to the task of identifying myself in a simple and
precise manner on a 1¾ x 2¾ card left me with only one option: to leave the

card entirely blank, refusing to attempt an honest answer, or with a simple line that said, "Anselm, CEO." I could not do either of those things, however, because each had been done so many times by so many other dorks that to do so would no longer have the intended effect of triggering the infinite, the complex and indefinable, but rather would only appear stupid, lazy, and dull. I wasn't aware of other men who become so paralyzed over such a simple task as ordering business cards, but Astrid had always stubbornly refused to see my perspective and had an endearing habit of badgering me until I relented. I let her create my business cards however she liked, her way. That was why my last batch had said, "Anselm Betty, eye blacker-outer," and why I was locked in my office right now, not crying, not tearing my hair out, but just sitting up straight, hands in my lap, eye darting across the room and finally landing on the reflection of my pen in my dark wood desk, and staying that way for hours. My inner Kafka was picking his nose.

Those quick to judge and anyone in the media might have put the past sequence of events together something like this: Annabelle's husband calls Zoë's husband and finds that both sisters have left town simultaneously and, jealous men that they were, they immediately suspected me for stealing them away and began sowing large red A's onto their wives' blouses. They called and informed the papers, and the next morning a scandalous report comes out. Astrid reads her morning paper while putting on a kettle of hot water, and, seeing the headline, drops the paper and runs upstairs to get her cell phone so she can call me. Dialing furiously, she dashes down the stairs, trips, and falls to her death, skull smashing into marble slab. Minutes later, the paper she dropped onto the stove catches fire and the whole house goes down in flames. This being merely the speculation of an amateur reporter at this point, he begins to doubt the believability of the paper on the stove (for who would be so careless?), and slightly revises the narrative to instead involve a twist at the end where rebellious teens from Willchester (teens who grew up in a household that had been negatively effected by something I had done at some point, something evil and uncool, and the teens therefore felt that they might somehow gain parental approval and be rebels in one fell swoop) got drunk, wore ball-caps, hung off the back of their unregistered trucks, and lobbed lit bags of shit onto my porch, sending the house, again, into a heap of malodorous flames.

What reporters don't realize, however, was that this story (take your pick of the two versions), however malicious and drenched in motivation and justice that it was, was not nearly as frightening as the horror of random, nonsensical, coincidence in broad daylight. They would never follow a lead where their only tips were a small, practically invisible, mention at the back of an independent weekly of a celebrity sighting in Little Anhedonia with his two friends, an electric fire caused by faulty wiring, and the vomit-induced death of an unknown secretary at her employer's residence while he was out of town. These things happened every day. A day that went by without these inconsequential, mindless, events that have so quickly ruined my life, would not be a normal day.

Yes, I'm fine, thanks.

If anyone at all actually deserved an honest response from me when they asked how I was doing, how I was holding up, they would not hear about the tormented mornings I had spent alone in a plastic blue chair in a cheap hotel room drinking scotch and crying into my collar as I flipped through sitcoms (although I did participate in this activity out of my well-bred sense of duty), no, they would instead cringe to hear that, despite it all, I have not felt this alive, this real, in a long, long time. No, I would say, Anselm was not fine, he was great. At eighty-nine years old, I was finally going to make some changes in my life; in fact, already had. My two cats, Jude and Francie, however, had not had the chance, and I missed their feline demonics already.

CHAPTER 24

Four double scotches before noon, I clicked off the TV/VCR and slung my lap-top bag's strap over my head and remembered to take the key card to the front desk before taking the next train to Willchester. I was enjoying music again, I realized, as I hummed along to the commercial jingle that accompanied the announcements of upcoming stops, even as I sat cross-legged between two aer-obics instructors. Disembarking, I took a longer route than required to get to the post office where I opened a new security box account and deposited one of the five folders.

The cool swish of the White Building's doors, an elevator ding, and the stale lemony air that filled our topmost floor all greeted me like the old friends that they were. Fine, thanks. I had plenty of time to spare so I swung by Simon's office and knocked before entering—a courtesy I had never before bequeathed. What can I say, I was feeling generous, kind even.

He looked up from the door's knob as it swung inward, and noticed his eyes were wide with surprise. He said I had lost weight. He was preoccupied with his own agenda, but quickly regained himself when I sat down in a leather chair by his desk and told him not to worry, that I was no threat to him any-more. What made me think that I ever was, he asked, closing windows on his computer as he stood hunching over it. He sat down, what made me think that I ever was, he asked again, adding that it had never been like that at all. It had never been like that. I changed the subject, thanking him for agreeing to the new requirements a couple weeks ago. He changed it back.

Simon, look, I have in this bag the beginnings of a project that will make you the richest man in the region, not to mention the most powerful. I have lived my life, it would be no exaggeration to say that I could die any day now, of natural causes, despite it all. I was prepared to use the remainder of my days to help someone else out for a change. I had changed, I told him. In any case, let's talk after the meeting, just you and I, and we'd make some plans. He was a good man, and we had had our disagreements, but that didn't make one of us wrong, one of us bad, did it? Simon folded his large hands into a steeple, then slammed the palms onto his dark wood desk and said, "You're a riot, Anselm, a bloody riot. And you've been drinking. A lot."

Simon stood from his desk and pulled at the collar of his brown suit and motioned me to the door. He grabbed my hand tightly and shook it, "Tell you something, Anselm. I say this out of respect, a deep respect for you and everything you've done. Why don't we cancel this meeting today, and instead, let you go home, or, go back to your hotel room, wherever, I'm sure you've got nice accommodations set up for yourself, and take a little break. Lots of things have happened, and we don't expect you to force yourself to continue to come to work like this. We *want* you to take a break, to rest, to recover, to think of yourself for once. Please, it's for the best. We will still be here in another week, another month, even another year. If you want to come back then, there will always be an office for you here. Always. Here's the elevator. Just take it downstairs, take a cab back to your place, and give me a call in a week or a month or two, however long you'd like. You'll see, after a little rest, you will thank me."

I stepped into the elevator, thinking it would be best to do things on his terms without making a scene, and I let the doors close, almost. I changed my mind and hit the buttons, and squeezed back out the chomping doors. Simon, this isn't right. Let's have that meeting first, and then you can decide what should be done after that. No? This is my company, Simon, it is my business. The meeting first. Don't do this. Get out of my way. Okay, okay, fine. This is silly, Simon, really silly. Although, well, never mind. Never mind. Oh well. I would not let go of his hand, he had to pry my fingers off. I've got a grip.

I took the elevator down one floor and exited. It was one of the many floors dedicated to developers, customer service reps, and human resource resources, floors that all looked alike and which I rarely saw. Cubicles spanned the wide open space with high ceilings, and in each square of space sat one of my many unhappy employees. The lights, carpet, and walls were of a cheaper material than was used on the floor above. I asked one of them if they knew of a staircase, and she pretended not to recognize me and directed me towards a certain corner of the room. Deciding not to be rude, I asked what she did. She was a software developer. What was she working on? Chance 2.0, mostly. Did she enjoy it? It was okay. What would she rather be working on? A novel. Really?

Yeah. Why didn't she work on that now then? Doesn't pay. I told her that was silly, and gave her my card (the last one I had) and told her to call me sometime tomorrow and we'd work something out. As a thanks for directing me to the stairwell. She commented on my title. That's correct. Perhaps I was flirting with a girl one fourth my age because she reminded me of Astrid, or perhaps it was because I was already thinking of ways of undermining Simon's latest move. At the very least I knew it was not because I actually cared if her damned novel ever got written.

When I entered the stairwell I found that my key card would not let me back in at the floor above where my office lay. Nor would it let me back onto the floor I had just entered from. Stubbornly refusing to believe that they had turned my key card off so quickly (for that must be proof once and for all that Simon really was trying to take my chair and that I wasn't being completely unreasonable by trying to get into the door in the first place), I stood in the stairwell for a number of minutes, hoping that someone might chance upon me here and escort me to my desired floor. As if engineered to be an elaborate joke at my expense, I slowly realized that I would not be able to enter my floor again without proving myself wrong. It was like a witch trial. If I was able to gain access to my floor it would've meant that they had not taken every measure to ensure my absence from that very floor, and therefore I wouldn't be able to accuse them of doing so. I tried each door on the way down a hundred flights of stairs, and did not find one that opened until I emerged outside the building on the ground floor. I determined then that I would need to plan my next move more carefully.

CHAPTER 25

I counted my steps from the White Building to Café Quine, over ten thousand; I must've skipped a whole bunch of numbers somewhere along the way, because the two buildings were not nearly that far from one another. I would not be surprised if I were off by an order of magnitude regarding the number of steps. I walked back to the White Building from Café Quine, counting my steps again. Each step was a cycle of pain and relief: pain as weight was lifted onto a single foot, and relief as the weight settled again on the two points in space. Even the relief was a little painful. Willchester was a shambles as per usual. I spent perhaps fifteen minutes between East Yale Loop and Kalen Court, for example, shuffling from pain to relief, from one hundred and nineteen to four hundred and seventy-three, ample time to shake my head at the multi-story buildings that had old brick shops on their first level, and horrid turquoise wood-panel apartment buildings dropped right on top of them. Buildings stacked upon buildings, Grey planning in a nutshell. And there were idiotic inconsistencies between neighboring blocks where some signal lights would use "WALK/DON'T WALK" signals and others would use the more modern hand/walking man. It was glaringly bad, as if the city planners had intended to make their process of ill-funded, mismanaged project cycles transparent to the user. The sidewalk occasionally angled sharply against the street, forcing the citizen to make blind turns onto busy streets. Damn. I think I was on 1,625, but it could've been 2,615. I kept both numbers, knowing that if I continued with my best guess, at the end I could see if it made more sense to add 990 to the final result. A shambles. I nicked my leg on a stone wall that I had walked too closely to and now my shin was bleeding. The blood seeped through my tan slacks just barely before drying up. I liked these pants, and would have to get Astrid to buy me a new pair. I was coming up on the White Building again. I had four numbers: 10,623, 9,633, 7,445, and 12,010, and think maybe my first count had been right. Since my original intention had actually been to visit Café Quine and talk with Anthony over a glass of red wine, I began counting my steps one more time, but lost count when I realized two things: that I had entirely forgotten about Astrid's funeral, and that Café Quine wasn't in Willchester.

Touching upon the same theme as the lost numbers and the lost appointments and being just plain lost, I could not figure out how the night had come so quickly. Lost time. I had just left Simon a few hours ago, taken a walk, hurt my leg, and now it was night. What had I done the rest of the time? Then it hit me: I was falling apart, I was losing it, and I was currently at that waypoint that one feared to ever cross, that point where one was aware of one's own mind deteriorating, even as that awareness itself deteriorated. I could cross that event horizon where all such self-awareness disappeared and I spent the rest of my life in a care home any minute now. Or maybe I was just stressed. The image of flat cardboard people walking past me and the cartoony flap of the hotel signpost as light and laughter echoed out of the jarred door did nothing to reassure me. I fell asleep on another rented bed with a framed self-portrait of Frida with some corpses over my head, and with my arms limp by my side.

Despite the promise to leave one another alone for a while, for time to heal if that's what it did, I called Annabelle early the next morning and, after asking her husband to wake her, began to communicate my numerous worries to her. She scolded me for calling, of course, still half asleep, and quickly agreed to call me back in an hour or two. I got Zoë's machine and left a lengthy note about how the step count had gone awry, and my bleeding leg. I called Skip Winters and finally had a human voice to talk to, and one whom I was willing to pay to have sympathize with me.

For five hundred dollars an hour Skip first accepted my rambling introductory story (was losing confidence in mind, now wanted to make sure I had someone to take care of me should I completely lose it, etc.) and offered some sound legal advice (update the will, sign a few papers that legally assigned power of attorney to another individual should certain unfortunate events take place). It was a little different than usual, he admitted, since I had no living family, nor children, but I was by no means in a position to have to worry about this too much. He told me I had made quite a fortune for myself and would therefore never be lacking attention and care. That almost cheered me up. We made an appointment for later in the day. It was not until Zoë called shortly after I hung up with Skip that I was able to formulate a reason to myself not to completely let go. I put on the same blood-stained classic tailored tartan tweed style suit that I wore yesterday, and the day before, and muscled on my Salvatore Ferragamos, and stood in front of the mirror and eyed myself over the crooked bridge of my nose. I saw everyman. I tucked my all-consuming empty signifier handkerchief into my front pocket and waited, waited for the next non-event to occur.

The triple-rap-tap of Zoë's knock awoke me and when I looked at her through the room's peephole (something that was easier now that I only had one eye), I saw a beautiful woman with a large center—the fish-eye lense pulling her extremities around its concave surface—holding a new suit in her right arm, looking at me knowingly right through the door. We lay down on the bed together, holding one another. It was quite painful for me but I did not want it to end. She explained to me the current situation with her husband.

Zoë's long black spiral-bound hair fell across her paper white skin and thick framed glasses. She looked up, pulled her hair back, and sighed. Her husband, does he need a name?, received a call from Annabelle's husband and, comparing stories, together discovered the adulterous plot against them (discovery here indicated with the palm of Zoë's hand as it flipped palm up over her hip). A wide hand-sweeping arc of inclusion summarized the collective reaction: complicated. Zoë was so close to me I could feel her words bouncing off my face. The sound level was almost null, most communication taking place with gestures and facial expressions. Her husband was a frustratingly sweet and patient man, and had heard Zoë out to the end, finally forgiving her for lying about her little stay in Little Anhedonia. She kissed my cheek, and rolled to her back, closing her eyes. The pressure created by propping myself up on my elbow had encouraged burning in my chest and sharp shooting pain in my shoulders, and yet I didn't feel it would be appropriate to relax just yet. Define happy. Define desire. I felt like a high school boy who had fallen in love with his teacher, and even though that metaphor failed on many other levels, it felt right.

My mind panicked and spun on metaphors when confronted with unsolvable riddles. One expectation I've always kept of this universe is that there must always be a way out, even if it was an illusion, even if it required re-writing the puzzle, or the rules, or just plain breaking them. Here, Zoë was trapped in a cage that, if broken, would harm her as well, and even if she should free herself, I was still trapped behind my pathetic inability to decide between two perfect sisters. It was ridiculous, just choose one. If Zoë and Annabelle were transported to a hypothetical scenario where a killer had a gun to both of their heads, and I was forced to choose between killing Zoë, or killing Annabelle, or killing both, but did not have the option of killing neither, what would I choose? I could kill myself (presumably leading to both of their deaths), or refuse to answer (presumably leading to both of their deaths), or attack the killer, or any number of fourth unspoken meta-options. Fine. In truth, the only answer was to forget the daydream. Destroy the scenario, erase that problem from the Book of Laws, wake up. Sure, they call it a rhetorical question, and it's rather presumptuous of myself to liken receiving the privilege of marrying me with getting your mortal coil shot through the back of your head, however, only more reasons to discontinue the daydream, only more reasons to fear what dreams may come.

Zoë pulled me on top of her, kissing me and hushing me, but whatever might have happened was cut short when my leg began to bleed again and I was forced to spend half an hour in the bathroom cleaning up. Clenching my teeth, trying to tear up, sure, but also cleaning up.

CHAPTER 26

Annabelle called shortly thereafter and met Zoë and I at the Andom Bay Dock Street station. She had on all her modeling makeup, and had an extravagant brown fake fur coat on over her presumably outrageous dress. She asked what had ever happened to my family, if they had said goodbye, or if they had been in the house during the fire. I realized that I had not thought of them once since leaving for Little Anhedonia several weeks prior. They did seem to have up and disappeared without a trace. Perhaps they hypnotized us and all the residents of Andom Bay on their way out in order to erase memory of their traumatic whirlwind visit in the first place. All the better, all the better I said, and anyway, who really cared. Forgetting that signified nothing, it was perfectly normal to forget one's family, if only it was so easy for others.

We took an early dinner with Skip Winters while signing the myriad papers that he had brought at my request. Annabelle and Zoë would be my witnesses tonight and the people who would have legal power of attorney over me should I fail to answer nine out of the following ten questions correctly five days in a row:

1) What is your name?
Anselm Douglas Betty

2) What is one plus one?
Two

3) What year were you born?
1912

4) Who is the President of the United States?
Georgey Porgey

5) What sound does a cat make?
Meow

6) What expression does one make to indicate happiness?
A smile

7) How many living siblings (brothers and sisters) do you have?
None

8) Name the three colors on a street light.
Red, yellow, and green

9) How many sides does a square have?
Four

10) Where are we right now?
The Glass House (variable)

I was permitted to study the answers all I wanted, up to within one hour of the test each day. We practiced over wine, asking one another similar questions, and threatening to lock one up should anyone ever answer wrong. How many fingers does a cat have? Eight. What was the average life expectancy for a single woman in 18th century England? 31. What sound does a duck make? Quack. What spot did Andom Bay get in *Kismet's* "Top Cities to Live In" survey? Third. How many sides does a triangle have? Three. How many women has Anselm loved in his life. Three. In your lifetime, how many cities has you lived in for longer than a year? Three. What was Skip's favorite number. Seven. We told him we were going to lock him up for breaking the streak. What was the source of wild passion according to the people in the Middle Ages? The spleen. Who invented the modern detective story? Arthur Canon Doyle. Which of these was not a cardinal sin: lust, greed, vacationing in Little Anhedonia. How slimy was Simon? What would the bill·come to? Who would get his just desserts, it being only a matter of time? And so on.

We signed the papers, agreeing to have either Annabelle or Zoë call me each day to ask me my questions. They both promised to report to Skip if I should fail five days in a row, or if they had any other questions about the questions, or wanted to change any of them. Zoë and Skip returned to their respective homes and Annabelle stayed with me for an afternoon dessert. She and her husband had had the talk, and it had not gone well. The husband had asked her to leave, had asked for a divorce. Did she explain that nothing happened? Yes. Then why? Because she admitted to loving me. She had? Yes. She did? Yes. My fork missed the cake three times before finally slicing off a portion, although I could not eat it. Perhaps the only thing that prevented me from having a heart attack was my patient resolution that I would definitely have a heart attack any moment now. Like the drunk man who survived the horrible drunken accident because he was too incapacitated to panic, and his body literally just bent like a reed and figuratively flopped like a blade of grass rather than breaking, I pulled the glass of water to my mouth, and slowly sipped, sipped so slowly, and did not spill.

We could get married in Anhedonia, I had friends who would do that for us.

"Zoë, Anselm, Zoë. We'll figure it out."

Annabelle stood and walked over to me, pulling my head to her tightly wrapped coat, and I glimpsed her bright orange dress underneath. She kissed the top of my head and excused herself, saying that she had to get back to work, she was in the middle of a shoot and did not want to ruin her makeup.

CHAPTER 27

I got on the phone the next day and made a few calls, taking the temperature of the city before making my move. The Andom Bay Company was busy addressing many of the Relevant Billboard problems that Chance Industries and Handsome Advertising had neglected to resolve beforehand. For example, would the billboards be two sided? Some people thought so, others didn't. The first batch had not been two-sided, and so The Andom Bay Company believed that none of them should be. Handsome Advertising, on the other hand, could sell twice as many slots with two sides. Chance Industries didn't care, as their software could handle either decision. Also, how important was it that the full network of billboards be released before Christmas? Fifty were deployed now, and businesses had so far been reluctant to purchase ad space, not accustomed to this new channel of advertising yet. If Handsome Advertising wanted two-sided billboards, the full deployment of the final fifty would have to wait until after the holidays, as they just didn't have the resources to alter the product and launch in such a short time. I asked them how much it would cost to complete before Christmas. They said it wasn't a question of money, but of time. Money was time if you used it to hire more people. But to train them as well? Poach from companies that already had the necessary talents. It wouldn't work. It would work, they just weren't thinking about it right. That got Chief Engineer of Development and Deployment Davis upset at me, and I hung up without trying to convince him further. Didn't I sign his paycheck, or hire someone who did? Twice in two days I had been blatantly defied by my own reports, and it was not an enjoyable experience. Perhaps it was for them, that was my only hope.

I wasn't able to make contact with the City Council reception desk, the primary number of their office had been disconnected with no forwarding number. My guess was that someone had changed a law and neglected to clean up after themselves. Sloppy play. The location and phone number laws were typical laws to change when superstitious members of the board felt that the current accommodations were causing bad luck or bad karma with their voting results. It had happened more times than I cared to count, and did not necessarily indicate that they were trying to hide from me.

I started calling people on the senior management team with the intention of finding someone who was willing to schedule a meeting with me and assist in arranging an opportunity for interested parties to listen to my new project idea. Chief Architect Yasmine's voice mail let me know she was out of town during this business week. Chief Algorithms Officer Andreas answered his phone, but did not have time to talk, promising to call me back in half an hour. Chief Mathematician Kurt was a little more promising at first, saying things were different at the office, not as good he said, but he hoped I was recovering smoothly. When asked about the meeting he declined, politely, saying that unfortunately he was unable to help there. Why? Just unable, he was really sorry. What? What was Simon doing? Really sorry. I got voice mail for Chief Engineer Michael and Chief Experimenter Meredith as well. After that, my phone got the busy signal for all Chance Industry calls. I rubbed at my stiff calf with the wound, thinking of the walk I was going to have to go on now. Knowing my current situation, I probably wouldn't get there before nightfall. I tried one more number, Senior Vice President of Media Outlets Tara, and Simon answered the phone.

"Anselm. How are you doing? Resting?"

One meeting. What was he afraid of? Would I come into his precious building and convince everyone to join my side, to throw him off his ill-earned throne?

"One meeting?"

Thirty minutes was all.

"Thirty minutes?"

Thirty minutes.

"Then what?"

Then I left him alone.

"Unlikely."

Then we'd see.

"We'd see."

Well?

"Alright. One meeting. One week from tomorrow. Noon. 8th floor A/V room."

That's it? Idiotic sentence fragments? Wasn't he going to hang up on me now with a few harsh parting words?

"Don't be a fool." Click.

CHAPTER 28

I rented the small one-room shop next door to Café Quine, a square abandoned lot with three white walls and a cement floor. The wall facing the street
was a grid of thin windows from floor to ceiling that weren't capable of stopping the wind from blowing right through them. I set up a dark wood desk in
the back corner, and spent nine to five in my tweed suit designing new business
cards and trying to think of a new name for my new business. Upstairs from
the office was a studio apartment with a bed, which I took to sleeping in. By
the time the painters came on the third day, I had a little design on a note card
which I asked them to paint on a square of space above the windows on the
outside of the shop. It was my best drawing of my own face, smiling. Anselm's
Smile. When I arrived at the office the next morning, I swept the cement floor
of debris, brushing it out onto the street, then propped the door open with a
stopper and washed the tall windows—outside, then inside. Then I sat at my
desk. Nobody came in, which was just as well since I didn't know what I
would've said.

In addition to the desk, I placed two wooden chairs along the back wall for
when Annabelle or Zoë visited. They were kind enough to not bring posters,
plants, office supplies, or baked goods. I made sure to get one question wrong
each evening: Andom Betty, Anselm Bay, zero, and this face. Dancing circles
around the flames of memory loss was not entirely unenjoyable.

There was a man across the street, lying prone on his belly underneath a
white van, snapping pictures of me. The next day my photo was in the paper,
"Anselm Betty, Still Smiling." The article was not flattering, and I did not know
the author. It cited certain fabrications in an almost playfully naïve way: I was
sleeping with two married women, I had tried to break into my old office

building, I was planning on faking my own death in order to trigger certain hidden statutes in the Book of Laws, I had opened up a new business and was slowly going insane in a chamber of my own devising—a bare room with no furniture, a store with no product, a life with no meaning. Anselm Betty is seen here sitting in his empty shop on Incomplete and 1st, which is curiously named Anselm's Smile. No doubt Daniel and Simon not only encouraged such amateurish journalism, but had also timed said article to debut on my presentation day. Attention reporters, break this man. I tucked the paper under my armpit, pulled my laptop bag strap over my head, and locked the shop door behind me, which had a sign in the window saying, "Out to Lunch."

The Relevant Billboard outside my shop was currently playing an advertisement for itself. Una Shin appeared on the screen, sitting on a picnic blanket in a green rolling field, and said, "Advertise your relevant business in a relevant way. Relevant Billboards, the best way to communicate with your customers in the 21st century. This special introductory offer will not last!"

I read a couple more articles on the train to Willchester, but could not recall their subjects even as I read them, for I was too distracted by the persistent thought that I should be mentally preparing for my GoldenScript presentation. The problem was that I had lost that complex mental construction of logic and purpose that had been created and fed by my own hand, and which had grown to enormous and healthy proportions˙ during my stay in Little Anhedonia. This mental construction had been equipped with presentation ideas, statistics, a clear vision, and confidence. I was not aware that such things could just disappear, but during my idle week where I set up Anselm's Smile, it had. Put another way, I was not on my game, and I knew it. Political and social figures can always tell when a meeting was doomed from the start. Signs were given to me. For example, I could not, even if I concentrated briefly, think of a way to open the meeting. Ladies and gentlemen. Friends and family. Coworkers and co-conspirators. The sound of the train's repeating melody was out of tune. Breathing and smiling and sitting up straight exhausted me, it was an effort to move the muscles in my face. I was confusing oranges with blues. A man not on his game was a doomed man, for office politics were not kind to the weak or the unprepared. Typically I cancelled such meetings, but for the first time in my life canceling the meeting was not an option, or rather it would be just as suicidal as botching it up in the worst way. Time moved unforgivingly forward and I lurched off the train and up the block to the White Building. People, power hungry entrepreneurs much like my old self, waited for these days to dawn on their foes, they were willing to wait years, decades even, for the irreversible signs of weakness, for the falling of the leaf, for the big bad boss to go out of style. My father, Victor and Jack Grey, these men had fallen, why shouldn't I? I was a hesitating fool. If I had my way I'd ascend these steps for the next ten years, hand permanently held out at this limp angle, passively reaching for the door's handle but never knowing precisely when two-dimensional hand would touch two-dimensional metal. At the same time, ten years was not a huge exaggeration, considering my current lumbering pace. My steps were not extremely quick, I was certainly not fast footing it to the top of these stairs. Nine and a half years later, Chief Mathematician Kurt came up behind me and took my elbow and escorted me into the building, mumbling behind his massive gray beard that it was a beautiful day, that his wife had made him the most delicious of breakfasts. And how was I? Fine, thank you.

The lemony scent of the 8th floor invaded my nostrils once again, and I could feel my grip on Simon's hand, and I could feel Zoë's words bouncing off my face, and I could feel the knife pushed up to its hilt in my socket, and I could feel myself pulling back in that typical Anselm way, recoiling in the cage from an attack, and then, like a pony with only one trick, like putting hammer to knee, like a ballerina that trips at the exact same step in her routine each time, like a spy that blurts his deepest secrets in his sleep at night, I flipped (indicated with the turning of the palm over her hip) and clung to that which was most comfortable to me, to the train, to my dark wood desk, to the brown coat, to sarcasm, trickery, and self-destruction. And I did it all while stepping into the 8th floor A/V room, one step behind Chief Mathematician Kurt, and if my facial expression changed at all it was only because I was preparing myself to destroy the only thing I had ever loved, myself.

Good morning, clowns. Let me get to the point. Simon has promised me thirty minutes of your time, and in that time I'm supposed to convince you that despite my missing eye, my bleeding leg, my adulterous tendencies, my quickly diminishing mental capacities, my utter lack of morals, principles, and even the potential to care, that you should continue to let my key card access this building. Sure, I'm still CEO, I still own 51% of the company, I still sign your paychecks, I still provide the good ideas, and the discipline to tell you when you're doing everything wrong, but what does that mean in today's city anymore? An old man needs his rest, you think. You all sleep for me. You think a crazy man shouldn't be allowed to run his business into the ground? They say ashes to ashes and dust to dust. How many of you believe in the afterlife? Can you think of any reason, seriously, as rational men and women, why I shouldn't take this gun out and shoot each one of you and then myself? That woke you up, Simon, did you really think I had a gun? Nifty. I've been watching the news, and things like this happen every day. We're not like those silly Egyptians, right, who thought that they could take their jewelry and mummified cats to the world after this, are we? Is this it? This is it folks. Must it be? It must be. I woke up scared this morning, scared, terrified of losing everything I had to Simon's political hot-footing, as he was basically using all my own trickery against me. Did I have any right to complain? Nope. Was I getting just what I had deserved all these years? Certainly. Does that mean I have to actually let it happen? Absolutely not. I have, in this folder a business case, technical spec, and schedule for a project that could take Chance Industries into the next century. The requirements document is in a safety box somewhere, and I planned to tie myself to the project so tightly that it could not succeed without me, essentially ensuring that the company would see to it as best they could that I survive long enough to benefit the company. Because no company can think of anything other than itself, and is constantly trying to factor out unnecessary elements (and I admit, at this point, without this bomb on my chest I would be an unnecessary element), these drastic measures were necessary. Because I did not want to destroy a lifetime of work merely to extend my own during these last few struggling and embarrassing moments, I could not force the company to do anything unless it was also in the company's best interest. But, you see, this is crazy talk! Crazy talk! Watch me lick this desk. Watch me kiss Simon on the lips. My mouth feels more defiled after the second than the first. Is there any difference between someone who chooses not to abide by any rule of society and someone who is crazy? I'll tell you what. Simon, you step down as Chief Scientist or I will destroy this company. Every single one of you will be unemployed by New Year's Day. I'm not going to fire you because I'd rather have you choose. It makes me happy to see you thinking. Simon, why don't you come by Anselm's Smile sometime in the next couple days and we'll talk. If I don't hear from you before next Monday, I'll assume that's because you'd rather see Chance Industries go the way of the sock puppet.

I tossed the three folders into the center of the table and walked out. Simon smiled back at me, his eyes like a kid's, excited and happy. Break this man.

CHAPTER 29

Annabelle, Zoë, and I had dinner in my upstairs studio that night. Cheers, to Andom Bay. Cheers, to Anselm Betty. Cheers, to Chance. Even I could tell we were in a weird spot, we had created a strange environment for ourselves. A land of stalemates. A move in any direction would put the king in check. To love only Annabelle and her heavy coats and her outrageous dresses, only Annabelle and her striking beauty that forced her to walk around with a large hat over her eyes, lest men see and be stricken with fear, this move would go strictly against my love for Zoë. To love only Zoë and her twisting black hair and her hand motions, only Zoë and her scratchy smoky voice, this would go strictly against my love for Annabelle. To love both was illegal, to love neither was idiotic. The same question that haunted me decades ago haunted me still. Did stalemate ever cease to be stalemate? Was there a lounge on the other side of this purgatory where stalemates had resolved themselves like trick knots? There was now another stalemate in my life: if Simon stepped down from the company, the Chance 2.0 project would be ruined as nobody else at the company had enough expertise to take the helm in his absence; if Simon did not step down, I was now obligated to shut down the company and therefore Chance 2.0 would never be completed. Without Chance 2.0, I had no immortality. My life would've been like any other's, and my mental construction would die in my head without having been translated into a physical object in the world that goes on living after I have died. The only way to allow Chance 2.0 to live would've been to sacrifice my own involvement and let it become another man's product, another man's immortality. Cheers, to stalemate. We drank a lot of wine that night, Annabelle, Zoë, and I. We promised, as drunk friends do, to love one another always, and to never forget each other. Immortal we would each be, as long as one of us remained in this world. After that, who cared?

Anselm's Smile was spinning up and getting some media attention. Advertising was a large part of the vision that I had for this company. Annabelle referred me to a director friend of hers, the one who had done her most recent round of commercials for the campaign, and I hired him for a series of commercials for Anselm's Smile. The series was titled, "A Room Of One's Own," and for a couple days the film crew lived in my barren shop and filmed my desk, my two chairs, my cement floor, and my grid of windows. I asked Tim to record a few different voiceovers for the commercials, each of which said, "No product, no business plan, no employees, no explanation, no reason." During lunch hour on Friday, Simon popped his head in, and I asked him to take a seat on one of my chairs (careful not to move it, as it was placed there for a reason) and I would join him on the other. He sat uncomfortably on the chair, the tail of his brown suit catching on one of the rungs.

"I'm going to step down from Chief Scientist, and suggest that you take on my responsibilities until you can find a replacement."

Fantastic. And what will you do now, Simon?

"You'll be hearing from me soon. Why spoil the surprise?"

I looked out at the cameras (turned off), and workers (standing and eating and pretending not to be listening to this conversation), merely observing details but offering no opinion of them. Simon, I'm not angry with you for trying to kill me, I hope you're not angry with me for trying to ruin you. This is business.

"Two good men can disagree, can't they?"

We shook on it, and he excused himself from the set and like that I was again in control of my business, my doomed business.

CHAPTER 30

Monday was catch up day. Projects currently on the plate included Chance 2.0, Relevant Billboards, Project Two, and the newly spun up GoldenScript project, which they had taken the opportunity to run with using my documentation. I was impressed. I held a meeting with the Project Manager of each team for a quick informal presentation of current status and upcoming milestones, and told them I didn't expect anything super-fancy on such short notice.

I invited Chief Mathematician Kurt to accompany me to the Chance 2.0 project meeting, in the hopes that he would be able to become the new lead. Chief Technology Officer Jeff gave me a run-down of current beta-blocking bugs. There was some data loss occurring between certain boxes, and the cause was unknown. What percentage of the data was being lost? About three percent, he said, after running his finger down some spreadsheets. Significant, but not a beta-blocker in my opinion, downgrade this one to a post-launch fix. Okay, what else. Some of the boxes had faulty hard-drives, and we were waiting to hear back from our distributor about getting replacements. How long would that take? Sixty days. How many boxes had faulty hard-drives and how much did they each cost? About two thousand boxes, and they cost about eight-hundred bucks each. I told Chief Technology Officer Jeff that while $1.6 million was a significant amount of money, we had invested much more than that already. We should buy new boxes from a manufacturer we knew we could trust, and in the meantime wait for the other manufacturer to not replace them, but simply refund us the original cost. We'd be out some cash in the short term, but in the long term it wouldn't make a difference. What else? Were you following this Kurt? Okay. There were 144 open sev-2 tickets on the new software candidate, and 19 sev-1s. Were they here last weekend addressing these bugs? Yes. Had the number gone down? No. Tell them that the number needs to go down, that by tomorrow we should have only 100 open sev-2s, and 5 open sev-1s, even if new ones come up, and that they should all be gone by Wednesday. This should be our top priority right now. Let's shoot for launching this, bug-free or not, a week from today. There will be no more changes to the spec, and we will cut scope and increase resources to make this happen. No more of this wishy-washy perfectionist nonsense, okay? Jeff, okay? Kurt, okay? Fantastic. Fine. Let's schedule daily war team meetings through next Monday, include me in them as well.

The Relevant Billboards meeting was next, attended by Chief Algorithms Officer Andreas, Chief Experimenter Meredith, and Senior Vice President of Media Outlets Tara. They provided reports on the latest sales numbers, which were coming in much lower than originally scoped. Handsome Advertising and the Andom Bay Company were currently in debate about the two-sidedness of the billboards, and it looked like all existing billboards would remain one-sided, and all new billboards would be two-sided. The consequence of this was that no new billboards would be installed until after Christmas. This was absolutely unacceptable. What options did we have, they asked. I'll tell them what options. How were new advertisements being uploaded into the billboards? Handsome Advertising was sending them an hourly XML feed with new advertisements, which we propagated out using the older Chance 1.0 boxes. Well, it was simple then, just refuse to install new advertisements until all one hundred agreed upon billboards were installed. Say that it was not worth our time to support a system of fewer than one hundred billboards, especially since the current sales were not coming in as expected. The success of this project hinges on a certain threshold of billboards being out there. We could not continue to invest our time in this until that threshold had been met. Can you tell them that? Okay. When? At the next meeting tomorrow. Call them right now.

I took lunch in my office by myself, behind locked door, a spicy chicken sandwich with lots of Tabasco and a glass of water.

Project Two was being led by Senior Vice President of Communities Derek, and had grown out of the individual proposals of the senior management team that were submitted a few weeks back while I was absent. The proposals, requested by me, addressed ideas on how to bring Andom Bay up to the number two slot of the "Top Cities to Live In" list for next year. Senior Vice President of Communities Derek had a Power Point presentation that he had given to the Andom Bay Company last week and which he thought might serve well for this meeting as well. He had lost sleep over this project. The desired goal of convincing the editors of *Kismet* magazine that our city was indeed better to live in than Willchester was almost impossible to address directly, so I understood his frustration. Let's see what they had come up with first. Importing one thousand plants from around the world, thereby making the city a bit greener. They had narrowed down a list of potential tree candidates by evaluating them aesthetically (canopy size, deciduous vs. evergreen, foliage color), biologically (climactic suitability, tolerance to pests and diseases, tolerance to low soil oxygen levels), and functionally (availability, structural strength, usual life expectancy), and had ended up with twenty or so qualifying candidates. Trees made people feel calmer, Senior Vice President of Communities Derek pulled out the article for me. What else was there? Buy a football or baseball team. Probably out of scope of this project's budget, but it was definitely a sign that people were thinking in the right direction. A national commercial campaign, in coordination with local travel agencies who were willing to offer special deals for air and train travel, that highlighted the benefits to tourists. In addition, we would inject marketing materials directly into Willchester, hoping to grab a share of its tourists' wallets. In addition, our news channels could syndicate more positive stories to the national broadcasting network, hoping that good news coming out of Andom Bay might get this city on more people's radars. There were several others, not as good, like attacking the city's crime and unemployment rates, hoping that the benefits of that change would trickle down to the city's overall reputation. A fine idea, but it would take longer than a year for those benefits to be noticed. Also, lots of ideas for fairs and festivals, two things I had always despised. My feedback to Derek was that he should seriously consider the commercial campaign, and also expand it to include all of the proposed ideas that had been along the same lines, such as using Chance as a publicity gimmick for tourists by dumbing it down a little and providing simpler interfaces to its data. GoldenScript might come in useful here, so I scheduled another meeting with him later in the week. Derek was doing a fine job, and the project (despite only being tangentially related to the company as a whole) was off to a great start. The tree idea was appealing as well. Trees *were* calming.

My last meeting of the day was with Chief Engineer Michael and his two lead programmers to discuss the spin up of the GoldenScript project. Michael had made copies of my business case, technical spec, hardware spec, and schedule, and passed copies to his two leads and myself. They had the why, how, and when, and had assembled a team of thirty software engineers, four

designers, three system administrators, two hardware specialists, and one quality assurance engineer according to the schedule, but they were still missing a
crucial element: he needed the what. What, exactly, were they building? I gave
them the high-level first. At its core, GoldenScript was simple, it was merely a
verbal interpretation of the text-based ChanceTalk language. ChanceTalk was
the alphabet, and GoldenScript was the phonemes, the sounds of the letters,
words, and sentences. Not literally, though. For example, take this line of
ChanceTalk:

```
if (defined $incoming_data) {
        $self->send($incoming_data);
}
```

This line, in GoldenScript, was not "If left parenthesis defined scalar incoming data right parenthesis left curly bracket, object self method send left parenthesis scalar incoming data right parenthesis semi-colon right curly bracket."
That should be obvious. Nor, however, did it necessarily have to be, "If incoming data is defined, then send the incoming data to the children," though it
could be. This is because GoldenScript will be built on top of current language
recognition and speech parsing programs to translate multiple different phras-
ings of a sentence into single action. It could just as easily be, "When you get a
message, pass it on." And to retrieve messages, you would just say, "Read my
new messages." New unrecognized sentences will be collected and analyzed by
the software to create best guesses, which, if wrong, the user can re-phrase
until the correct action is taken. That correct action will then be associated
with the initial unrecognizable sentence for all future uses. Because Golden-
Script will be implemented in Chance 2.0, every Study Box that has the Golden
Box plug-in will be able to receive and send messages via GoldenScript. Golden
Boxes themselves will not be expensive, only slightly more expensive than standard Study Boxes, but they will not require a keyboard, and will give us a
chance to implement the user account facilities that are integrated into Chance
2.0 software. Every user will have a set number of account privileges that will
give them access to a certain level of data. The lowest account privileges will
not do much more than allow reporting of local statistics: GPS, temperature,
proximity of other boxes within 50 ft that have allowed their presence to
become known, text message sending and receiving, speech storage (which is
automatically translated into text), and remote connection to any other Study
Boxes that have granted them access (including any public Study Boxes). At the
highest user account level, you would have access to the density of people in

any location that has such measurements being recorded, high-level statistical reporting of traffic to any given area historically, access to data and remote control of all enabled computers and boxes on the network, reporting on which, if any, experiments you're currently taking part in, and this is all just the tip of the iceberg. As you all know, Chance 2.0 will have an application programming interface that will allow third parties to easily create software and other tools to access on the network. Freed of the keyboard and the graffiti pen, everything becomes machine readable and accessible to the average person without the hassle of having to learn a new language. Did that make sense? No answer. Does the spec make more sense now? Yes. Good enough for me.

If I had to guess, the general reaction of the employees to my return that day seemed to be favorable, if a little cautious. There was a shadow of a doubt in my head that crept across my vision of myself as a proud standing figure in the doorway of business. I felt that they had been watching me from a distance, not fully participating or engaging me in debate. Definitely much more afraid of me than they had been before. Not only judging my actions, but judging me. Yes, I am a paranoid man, and have several conspiracy theories to prove it.

CHAPTER 31

It was nobler in the mind to suffer the slings and arrows of outrageous fortune after all. Who the hell knew? Anselm Betty did. With my company back, especially after seeing it deteriorate to a rather pathetic state after my short absence, and for all to witness how I was able to get it back on track within a couple weeks, this was the validation that a well-lived life was made of! The return of a well-executed program. Chance 2.0 launched onto the streets of Andom Bay on Thanksgiving Day, and I led KWLT news correspondent Mary Cartwright through the basement of our headquarters, through the core bundle of ten thousand computers that served as Chance's brain. Not really, since there was nothing to distinguish these computers from any other computers on the network—they all ran on the same software, and had no hierarchy—but this was what the viewers wanted to hear. The entire network had been down for most of the morning due to an unexpected outage, but everything seemed to be blinking blissful robotic life now. Ms. Cartwright asked me to explain to the viewer the driving vision behind Chance. It was, simply, to make life measurable, recordable, searchable, and interactive, what we often refer to as "machine readable" rather than a jumble of sensations that can only be interpreted approximately through the senses. What we had before today was a world where very primitive mechanisms were set up to record the state of an environment and the change in an environment in real time. One example is how we use archaic technologies to determine which television shows are the most popular by watching a tiny subset of the viewing population, and extrapolate those results as representative of the entire population. Now, we can watch them all. And now we'll also know the breakdown of viewers by geographic area (dissected into units as small as neighborhood blocks), when they stop watching your show, and which show they're watching instead, etc. That's just one example, there are millions of others. Advertising can become smarter, people can become more informed of their lives through actual data rather than general impressions, and everyone can be more informed overall.

"Now, I'm sure you're aware of what some of your critics are saying, that this network is a slap in the face of privacy and security. They say that to put this much information into the hands of any one organization, one that is motivated by profits and not necessarily by what is best for the people, will only lead to abuse of such information. How do you respond to these accusations Anselm?"

I'm not forcing this on anyone. It's a one-to-one exchange. Only those that own information can decide if that information becomes public, and that hasn't changed. At the same time, two things are going to become clear fairly soon: one, that it turns out that most information is public, and two, that one must give information in order to receive information. Just because certain data has never been collected before, such as the relationship between the prominent display of signs and the effectiveness of those signs to prevent accidents on a city street, doesn't mean that it wasn't public information all along. Anything that doesn't relate to a specific individual or organization in such a way that their identity is compromised, is public. Same goes with most group behavior, the traffic in malls, the purchasing habits of certain demographics and geographics. Also, trust is going to be a big issue—in order to retrieve information from the network, you're going to have to give something back in order to prove that you're trustworthy. Identity and access to personal information is an almost flawless sign of trust. Sharing of information is one of the most important aspects in any relationship, whether it be between two people, two businesses, or two computers. I plan on leading by example on this front and making all my private information public. Once people realize that it's not really that compromising, that privacy is still enabled even at the most revealing level, I think more people will understand.

"Can you explain how this works?"

This is a Study Box. You can buy them for $199 at any of the authorized retailers in the area, and they'll serve as a portable wireless access point to the Chance 2.0 network. It comes with a lifetime subscription to the network, as well as the basic account that gives you access to all local information (that which your box is recording) as well as any information that has been given world-readable access, like library information, most information available on the Internet, and some retailers that have chosen to participate.

"It looks like a black box to me. How to you interact with it?" She spun it in her hands as if it were an unsolvable Rubik's Cube.

Well, right now, you need to hook this up to another device, be it a computer, PDA, or cell phone. We have another product coming out soon which will make these boxes interactive without that secondary requirement. For now, yes, it does require that you have some other device that has a keyboard or touchpad or graffiti pen.

"Do you have time to give a demo with this?"

We walked over to a small desk we had set up in the basement for this purpose. I jiggled the mouse on the computer to remove the screensaver, plugged a cord into the Study Box, and then, using the keyboard, typed in a line of code that would retrieve a map with the locations of all the attendees to my head unwrapping media event—a group that was still undergoing analysis. I punched the enter key. The screen went blank, an icon at the top corner of the page spinning furiously. We waited. I explained that the network still had a few bugs to work out, that this was to be expected on the day of the launch, but a week from now everything should be working much more smoothly. Better to launch early and get feedback than to wait forever trying to create the perfect product only to realize that the public wasn't interested. The page timed out and I got an error. I hit the back button and retried. Same thing. Hopefully, Mary would be able to edit this portion of the segment and I could send her a printout of the results. That would work fine. She changed the subject.

"And how many computers are there out there as of today, already gathering information?"

Approximately one million.

"And it all starts here, is that right? In the basement of the White Building. A lot of wires, blinking lights, and computers stacked floor to ceiling. I've never seen anything quite like it. I wish your product launch the best of success, Anselm. Chance 2.0, the end of privacy, or the beginning of a new machine-readable future? Only time will tell. Back to you, Scott."

I apologized for the glitch.

"It's all the same to me."

When the piece ran, I was told it had been truncated severely and ran only the very beginning and very end of my interview. It was just as well, since I had twelve more interviews in the next couple days anyway. I am not a perfectionist, I believe that perfectionists waste most of their time worrying about details, when it's the grand vision that counts, and that the public remembers.

The constant hum of stress in my chest had returned, a familiar friend that I had carried along with me during most of my years, one that put the spring in my step and the twinkle in my eye. Without stress, you have seen the man I become: one that worries and has second-thoughts and who locks himself in his room with a spicy chicken sandwich. Stress was a friendly adversary that helped me make decisions. For example, I had tried calling Una Shin for directions to the next City Council board meeting, but she had neglected to return my call. So I called Simon. Simon said that he didn't know, that he had had trouble finding it himself, but had not bothered following up on it since he had lost his position in the board after I had taken his place. I should've continued calling, I still hadn't tried Daniel or Kenneth, but stress advised me to let it be for a couple days. There was no hurry to get re-involved in that circle, as I had plenty of other things on my plate at the moment. In my younger days it hadn't been a problem, but as much as I loathed the thought, I now had to take into consideration my own health. Stress may have also had a part in my failure to answer nine out of ten questions correctly for the first time. I said Don Foster was my name, and that I was born in 1925. Annabelle thought I was playing around, and that I had missed the two questions on purpose, when in fact I had only missed one on purpose. I got them all right the next day, and then only one wrong for the following couple days, though these were the real deal, I was no longer playing around by giving one false answer. Each night, now, before Annabelle or Zoë came over, I would spend an extra hour looking over the questions and answers, how difficult could it be to burn these answers into my head? My name, for Christ's sake! I should know this by now. Are these the ramblings of a crazy man? Could a crazy man run a business, a city even? Certainly not. Therefore I was fine.

Christmas must've happened, because suddenly it was January, and then February. I was hospitalized twice for dizzy spells, nothing serious. Relevant Billboards were fully deployed and finally catching on with businesses. Anselm's Smile was a nice side project, but the commercials had been caught up in post-production delays and had not yet aired. I wasn't too worried about that. My name had been appearing in the news at a steady stream for the last couple months. Simon was a distant memory. My new enemies included privacy advocates and wimpy grassroots organizations, but they lacked the backing to do anything but protest and threaten to take me to court. I had a team of lawyers that I felt obliged to pay full time in order to keep those types of folks busy. I knew for a fact that I would never set foot in a courtroom, as that would be a waste of my time. At night, I enjoyed my sleep. I was waking up fully rested at 3am each morning. Chance 2.0 had been cursed from day one with technical glitches and extended periods of downtime, but had still managed to ignite the curiosity of neighboring cities, as tourism was up almost 35% year over year. A telling factor that we were doing something right was that rents on apartments had gone up 7% since last year in the city, and had been going down steadily in Willchester for several years now. Senior Vice President of Communities Derek had gone ahead (with my blessings) with his nation-wide commercial campaign, which included numerous references to Chance 2.0 and Relevant Billboards, as well as locally run advertisements on the Relevant Billboards themselves. His proposal for the tree implants was passed on to the Andom Bay Company, and they've since adopted it and plan on having a thousand new trees planted by the end of the year. Except for questioning sessions each evening, I had seen Annabelle and Zoë an ever decrementing number of minutes each day, which was more torturous than I felt comfortable admitting.

Then, one evening, after getting only six of the ten questions right, Annabelle told me that she and her husband had decided to have a separation. She held my two cold hands to the side of her warm neck and told me again that she adored me, and wanted to be able to spend more time at my side. It was like a movie. She knew I was busy, and she was busy too with her commercials (her presence in more demand ever since local businesses started creating commercials for the Relevant Billboards), but even if it meant two hours a day, or less, it was worth it. I agreed. I was thinking as much about my need for support in the near future as I was for anything else. Slightly monstrous of me, but the constant delaying of any decision making on anyone's part was beginning to get rather old, and so was I. If I was a decent man I would've pushed her away and let myself fall apart alone, or at least with paid, non-emotionally-tied, help. I wouldn't be dragging her into what I knew would be a rather pathetic and horrible firework display of morbidity for us all. I knew that what I was doing selfish, self-centered, and self-indulgent, I knew it all from day one. I believe that's why it felt so natural. I am not an angel. Doubters can refer to this tiny newborn sliver of a toenail that has recently emerged, blinking its bewildered eyes at me.

CHAPTER 32

I had a review session with an early Golden Box prototype, not in my claw-like hands as I would've preferred, but rather set up around me as an entangled collection of headphones, microphones, control panels, and monitors. They had not yet perfected the little golden cube that I had imagined to fit into the palm of my hand, apparently. Nothing was actually golden. For now all of the development efforts were being spent perfecting the language component for receiving and sending information.

As instructed, I placed the heavily padded headphones over my ears, and pulled the microphone close to my mouth. Chief Engineer Michael mouthed the words, "Say something."

My name is Don Foster.

"Ask it a question."

What's my name?

"Your name is Don Foster, you are the CEO of Chance Industries, The Andom Bay Company, and Anselm's Smile." The voice was robotic with the treble dial pulled all the way to ten, but I was still impressed.

How many people are in this room?

"Four. Yourself, Chief Engineer Michael, Lead Technical Programmer John and Lead Technical Programmer Jenny."

How many people in this room are participating in Study Box experiments?

"Two."

What is Simon Meany's cell phone number?

"Did you just ask if Simon Meany has any children?"

No.

"Did you just ask for Simon Meany's name?"

No!

"Please rephrase the question."

Chief Engineer Michael was motioning to take off the headphones. "Of course, there's still a lot of loose ends to wire up and data to upload to its memory, but this is a start. A solid start, wouldn't you say? We'll nail this project, Anselm. Give us another month or so, you'll see. You are a genius."

What would it take to install this prototype in my apartment? Was this computer accessible remotely? I plan on playing with it as it grows, consider it an opportunity for a constant feedback loop into the project. Of course he hesitated. Any decent program manager would, as it increased the potential for new requirements to get added while at the same time increasing the attention on the project and the pressure to meet dates. Of course, he had to say yes. We spent the rest of the meeting updating the schedule, and making sure this was still going to ship sometime this year. And I wanted it to be golden, and box-like, as soon as possible.

Chief Engineer Michael volunteered his help by boxing up some of the components and carrying them to my apartment for installation. My arms were no longer strong enough to handle a twenty pound box. We laughed about the increasing frailty that old age brings as we walked up to the windows of my shop and apartment. Annabelle and Zoë were inside and the room was dark except for a light descending from the stairwell door at the back of the room. It looked as if Annabelle was leaving, her body was directed towards us as she looked over her shoulder and took small hesitating steps. She was hurling short expletives to Zoë. She saw us standing outside, wiped her face, and rushed the door. I opened it for her, whereupon she made a small bird-like peep and then hustled off. Zoë ran through the stairwell door up to my apartment. I clutched my arm and thanked Michael for bringing this down. I would find someone to install it tomorrow. He placed the boxes against the window inside the shop, then bid me goodnight. Ascending the steps to my apartment, my mind recalled the image of Zoë and Annabelle on the couch in Little Anhedonia, and I mourned the passing of that moment with all the coherent fibers that were left in me.

CHAPTER 33

A momentary lapse in concentration as I ascended the steps to my apartment, where I could hear Zoë's muffled sniffs percolating down, gave the demons a perfect opportunity to catch up with me; they pricked me with the myriad painful inconsistencies in my story that I had written for myself. Who was I fooling? I knew who. When I reached my entry way, I hacked up dry air for a minute on my hands and knees, and prayed to Christ Almighty for a clean slate, a re-do of the last couple months, and a helping hand. I'm on my hands and knees! Yes, this was embarrassing, and perhaps a suspiciously childish attempt at bringing attention away from Zoë's worries by forcing her to focus on me instead, but it felt honest, real, and cathartic.

Zoë led me to the couch, half carrying me, my fragile limbs folding into the seated position. I felt strangely invulnerable, though, despite all the evidence to the contrary, and presented my most confident words of reassurance to Zoë that whatever it was that she and Annabelle had been fighting about, it would be okay, they would work it out.

During Zoë's ensuing monologue of many opinions and fears, she was strangely still. Her wildly motioning arms had been clipped, her many-expressioned face had been frozen. Something was wrong, something that went beyond the story of the fight with her sister. Zoë had learned through the paper that Annabelle had separated with her husband, and felt hurt. Felt that by not telling her own sister about it, she must have been hiding something. That something was me. I told her many times that I was fine, that the Golden Box prototype had been stunning, that Chance Industries had a momentum and excitement to it that it had been lacking for many years. She continually interrupted me, no matter how much I reassured her, until finally she wouldn't let me speak at all.

"You're not listening to me."

Of course I was.

"No, you aren't. You aren't listening to me."

Zoë removed her black coat and revealed a silver shirt underneath that sparkled and danced in my dark room like an ocean under the moon. There were several old Study Boxes installed in my apartment, they recorded simple things like temperature, light levels, moisture and sound, but they could not understand anything we were saying. Of course I am, Zoë, I am right here, I am listening.

She bent over on her hands and continued crying. She had already been crying, but she renewed that act by expressing it more publicly with her posture and the sound of her sobs. I wouldn't mind visiting the bay, seeing the moon dance on the water.

"No, Anselm, no. Can't you see? Can't you understand what I'm saying? Why can't any of it get through? Where are you Anselm? The bay, the bay, the fucking bay."

It would be okay. She did not normally act like this, something was clearly bothering her, but she would not say what. If Annabelle had been here she would straighten this out. The sisters cancelled each other out.

"Annabelle isn't helping you. She was lying, she was hurting you. Dear, she was making it worse for everyone! Do you know what she was doing? Do you have any idea what your best friend Annabelle was doing?"

I had met Annabelle first, many years ago. She had been wrapped up in a thousand colorful furs, a rainbow of artificial color and artificial taste, an ad on the side of forty buses that I had purchased for the city. I had met Zoë after Annabelle, they had both attended a party in the Willchester museum, a private party celebrating Victor and Jack's 25th anniversary. In a sense, Zoë had been catching up to her sister ever since, becoming closer and closer to being the first person in the door, at the coat-check, shaking my hand. Her hands, her voice, her color, a swarm of disconnected qualities that had tangled me up in their net, but maybe I had loved Annabelle first, and most.

"Anselm, listen to me."

I was.

"When's the last time you answered your questions correctly, Anselm? Annabelle has been telling us that you have been getting them correct every night. Have you been?"

I don't know. I don't remember. If I could run a business during the day, the most successful business in the city, did I really need to answer my questions one hundred percent correctly? There was a difference between being a functioning adult and one who had memorized a bunch of useless details that he could just as easily get from a calculator, or a secretary. The city itself had become my brain, my will, my memory, so why store redundant information in my own flesh when it was no longer necessary?

When I woke I was in my bed and Zoë was gone. My arms lay limply at my sides, and I was comfortable and warm enough that I did not think immediately of rising. Light sources that I could identify included a street light translated into horizontal lines of variable width by my blinds, the black glow of my computer's screen saver, and a pair of blinking red light sisters indicating the synchronized dreams of my clock radio. When I was a child, this morning hour before my parents woke would be the most frightening and dreadful of the day. The prison of privacy forced one to contemplate death and the slow march of time. And here it was so many years later, still marching, still inconceivably reliable. Was it indeed the same thing? Its patience and consistency and endless pace was an inspiration for madmen. I had done this enough to know that to think about it was to destroy it, so that I did. Fantastic.

My clock radio burped on precisely twenty minutes later, informing me of Chance Industries' new interim Chief Executive Officer: Simon Meany. Annabelle arrived shortly afterwards and folded the paper open for me on my bed: Anselm Betty Deemed Unfit to Run Chance Industries by City Council. Unable to answer ten simple questions correctly, the city had decided it was in my best interest to ask me to step down. Helping me into my classic tailored tartan tweed style suit, Annabelle apologized for the fight she and Zoë had had. Sisters fought. But she would not let it harm me, for she loved me more than love itself. She would be back in the evening, after work, and reassured me that everything would be okay. I told her the same.

I walked down the stairs with Annabelle, and saw three boxes slumped at the door right where Chief Engineer Michael had left them last night. Opening up the boxes and taking up first the bundle of wires, and then the microphone stand, and then the headphones, and then the microphone and cord, and then the connectors and adapters, and then card reader, I slowly emptied the boxes and rebuilt the Golden Box upstairs as best I could. I left behind the monitor, and one heavy metallic device, hoping that equivalent parts upstairs would work just as well. It was a time-consuming process to relocate and rebuild this physical object, especially since I didn't remember which inputs connected to which outputs, and my back couldn't handle the strain of bending over for longer than two or three minutes at a time without folding into constricting cramps. I floated on the soft red cushions of the couch for recuperation when needed, rebooting muscle and nerve connections. When every wire was connected, but the box still wasn't being recognized on my computer, the hobnobbing, rascally, little man called.

After the goodness of the morning was debated, Simon insisted on being resilient to my suggestions to give my company back. Not willing to waste too much time with this man, I hung up on him after getting information about the location of the next City Council meeting. I resumed the assembly of my Golden Box. My frustration manifested itself as a tangle of wires and an ignorantly blank screen. I smashed the screen and ripped the wires apart with my hands, or I would have if such strength were granted me. I might as well be tearing at my own face. I called Annabelle at work and she agreed to meet me on her lunch break, several hours away. Is an hour very long? My reference point was lost. Zoë arrived at my door right then, without prompting, and carried the remaining boxes up to my room. Within minutes she had solved the riddle of wires and plugs required to bring the box to life. I was doing something right to get such a stroke of luck. The game was favoring me at the moment, so I pressed further.

Did you tell them?

"That's why I came. I didn't. But now I see that with all of these boxes in your room recording every sound, smell, and change in moisture, I should've realized that anyone on the network could've been listening and reporting anything we said."

Where was the paper with the answers? I would simply start getting the answers right again and the company would be given back. Zoë's amazing memory determined that the paper's location was my wallet. Sure enough, I pulled a small business card out with ten questions and answers typed on both sides. I flipped it back and forth in my fingers, its lightweight two-dimensionality twinkled like a star.

CHAPTER 34

My name is Anselm Betty. One plus one is two. I was born in 1912 and the current President is Georgey Porgey. Cats meow, we smile when we're happy, and I have three living sisters. The three colors of a street light are red, yellow, and green. Squares have four sides and right now, right now I am in Andom Bay, a city of my own invention.

From there we leave solid ground, though what we have so far should get us through the tough spots. Everything that follows, though speculation, will nevertheless be presented as fact in the court of law. I am the CEO of two companies, one named Chance Industries, the other named the Andom Bay Company. I love two women, sisters by the names of Annabelle and Zoë, members of the family Mumford. I saw them both as recently as today, and am almost certain of their existences. Ninety-five percent sure. I am not a mad man. My life has been a series of orderly and predictable events one after the other, though you must realize that upon examination, any particular event can be scrutinized until it has zero probability of having actually occurred. No detail can pass the test of being considered within the set of all possible things. One could establish a reasonable doubt that any of these events which I vividly remember have ever taken place. Nevertheless, Willchester begat Andom Bay. Andom Bay begat Little Anhedonia. On a dusty shelf in one corner of Little Anhedonia Library lies the rejected proposal for the Good Willchester Correction Facilities. I walked through these three cities street by street, naming buildings, years they were put up, previous owners, current owners, relationship to other businesses in the area. I named parks, rivers, and hills, rolling up and down the Landscape.

I vomited up as many of the details that I could scrounge together, recording them digitally, not simply as sound but as live, machine-readable data. The Golden Box faithfully dissected, sorted, and indexed this information in me while I could still access it. It would be a perfect replica of my memory. I am currently in my apartment. Where are we right now?

"We are currently on the corner of 1st and Incomplete, in a studio apartment located above Anselm's Smile."

What is my name?

"Your name is Anselm Betty."

Who will win, Anselm or Simon?

"Anselm."

Fantastic. Of course, it didn't know the future, only whatever I had previously input into this machine. At the moment, it trusted that everything I told it was true, because there were no conflicting stories to make it doubt. Free-association led me from childhood games to the process of creating blueprints to the pattern on particular couches in Little Anhedonia to the miles of coastline along Andom Bay to the test results from our "No Jaywalking" experiment to cats to paintings to dirt fields. I assigned system-wide read privileges to this data and asked that it be stored in fifty redundant Study Boxes that were equidistantly distributed across the city. Write privileges would be limited to Anselm Betty himself. Should he forget who he was, he would be identified by voice recognition software which would be compared to an archived recording of Anselm's response to the command, "Say: 'My name is Anselm Betty.'" Having to make a three o'clock meeting across town, I tested the Golden Box three final times, verifying that my data was secure and properly saved, then locked the computer, locked my apartment door, locked the shop, and walked slowly, deliberately, helplessly, down the hill, forming an entrance strategy in my mind.

CHAPTER 35

When I listened closely on this tale of a clear winter day, even with these stale parched drums, I could hear the crunching and spinning of thinking computers. Billions of bits of data flowed through a billion thin pipes every billionth of a second. The street itself was a computer constantly computing its next state. Every pebble that was batted out of the way with my cane was forced to compute its next move barely in time to realize it. The street, every grain and crack, was merely a sub-process running within the larger computation of the entire city. It was this computational power that Chance had been originally designed to tap into. Chance would simply be yet another sub-process riding on top of the universal program. The main side effect of such a program was to constantly calculate the future, as the future was needed in order to calculate the more distant future, and that was needed to calculate the even more distant future, and thusly time moved forward and forward and forward some more. Given sufficient data and enough memory, Chance too could compute the future (as could any other computational device), although of course not fast enough to actually get ahead of the universe's computation of it. Computing shopping patterns and social networks, programming streetlights and elevators, that was one level of interesting data, and perhaps I had given people the wrong impressions about the end goal of this project and they thought that was it. I wanted this wind to be warmer. This moving sheet of air which rolled off the nearby mountains, chilled itself over the bay, then shot through downtown to reach my face here, had the incorrect settings all along. Where was the control panel for this wind?

A gaggle of Simon look-alikes shuttled up and down my street. Brown suits and tan coats wrapped around men and women who moved in random repetitive circuits like zombie processes. They nudged me as they passed, and one that apologized was scolded with my harshest invective. The sidewalks I had set were divided into square slabs of concrete, separated with half an inch of room to grow and shrink on warm and cold days without cracking. These sidewalks looked rectangular now, and were a blinding gray. Wash these sidewalks, Simon! Re-cut them! Buy new ones if you must. Sidewalks were a city's underwear. I walked by Café Quine, and wondered if Zoë had ever ended up playing her show. If so, why hadn't I known? If not, why hadn't I known? Information was not circulating properly, that was my point. When a system relied on an unreliable network of neurons and uncaptured vibrating air, and used stretched pads of skin to transmit and receive data, how could anyone be surprised when something got lost? If I had not created better forms of communication for this city than that, I would be the one to blame. But no, the wires were right here, the boxes were right there, I insisted on walking behind Anthony Dumont's cash register and pointing at the computer, linked up directly to Chance, which he could've easily updated with his shows to ensure that I, who was subscribed to nearly every data feed available (filtered and filed away into relevant buckets of course), would've known. She had played. Months ago. I spat on Anthony's table on my way out.

The cold wind was getting stronger, turn it off! Turn it off! There was no excuse for this treatment. Halfway across a street, the opposing lights turned green, and Simons honked and yelled from their windows. I stopped and looked at these plain faces through their reflective cases. Emotions distorted their expressions, and then didn't know how to proceed. Paralysis was part of the program. It was a valid move. They asked me what was wrong.

It's too windy.

I can't see downtown from here.

This stoplight should know I'm still crossing.

You are in my way.

This city is already falling apart.

Who will take care of you when I'm gone?

Now get back to work.

My company was taken from me and I'm going now to take it back.

I made this city but to what extent did I control it? More importantly, how much did I know about it? This orange building, it was built originally as a seed furniture store, planted here to encourage more furniture stores next to it. Furniture stores existed on a scale-free network which privileged the clustering of stores to a limited extent (about five within a couple blocks was found to be the optimal ratio, and then another cluster of five no closer than fifteen miles away). Owned by Harold, Good Furniture and Lighting now had twenty stores within this county and almost everyone owned a chair by them, or a lamp. In the beginning they had been plagued with a reputation for being cheaply constructed, but some aggressive marketing has all but reversed that stigma. I was a fifteen percent investor in the company and had first suggested to Harold that he furnish all of the local bookstores and cafes with donated pieces, a ploy which proved successful in making people comfortable enough to bring the shoddy product into their house, their home. No wait, this was the bath store, not the furniture store at all. This I didn't know who owned. That was a lie, I just didn't care. I buy all my bath products from the store on 5th and Proper, that store being much more well managed, by friends, this one being doomed to go out of business any day now.

I could always orient myself in the city by looking for the sister radio towers. They should've been to my right, as I turned onto an open street with a view, but they were not. White fuzz, brown clouds, and the noise of light bouncing at full computational speed was so distorting that I was not sure if I was looking in the right direction. Of course, without the orienting object itself, I could not know for sure whether I was looking in the right direction or not. I pulled the directions out of my pocket and shoved them in a passerby's hands. Tell me where I am and where I should be going. Where are the radio towers, am I going crazy or are they normally in that direction?

The stranger mumbled something, pushed the paper back in my hands, and moved along. Another did the same. The all-consuming Landscape was resisting this Agent. My will was probably stored on a computer somewhere not fifty feet from my feet, and in it was a map of the city. The lack of access to that information felt like the separation of a device from its outlet. My eye felt along the two-dimensional screen and tried to sense the presence of a key, a door, a clue of some sort. A curb and grate and a bush presented themselves, I moved on. My eye, finding a sign, could focus on the shape of the letters, then on the texture of the paint on the letters, then on the splotches of other-colored paint (what happened here?) and the scratches, and yet find no meaning in it. Which way was information stored, where was the socket, where the translator? Which process could remind me of my destination? I tried random messages, like "Bloody Simon, bloody blood blood," and "I love you," but I could decipher no knowing eyes, nor saving hands, in the abyss. The roar of computation rose up and drowned out my thinking, short circuiting the links between thoughts, abandoning floating bits in an alphabet soup, a dust pile, fallen leaves from a tree that could never be reassembled. Humpty Dumpty, a flooded ant hill, a crashed hard drive. For a split second, I believed and embraced the end, then yanked myself back up and out.

It was healthy to let oneself go like that occasionally, a single line of consciousness holding oneself up over a nonsensical bay, and then, at the last minute, the bungee umbilical cord pulling you back up, and you had wet toes, and your heart was racing, and you felt exhilarated and glad to be alive. Such was I.

I was collapsed in a medium-sized hedge when I came back, green eye-shaped leaves squirming between my armpits, into my ears, and between my legs. Branches snapped and crackled under my influence. A semi-circle of spectators looked in horror at the plant I had destroyed. Perhaps it was one of which Senior Vice President of Communities Derek had recently planted. Was this city now more green? Had the people noticed? Have you noticed more trees lately? More green things, like this, with leaves and sometimes a trunk? But they did not answer, for they had not noticed. Wake up, ants! It is your job to be aware of your surroundings, to take part in the city in which you live. We try to communicate with you, but if you aren't listening then whose fault is it? If our city doesn't make the top of the *Kismet* list, whose fault is it? Look over there, see any towers? No. Why not? Fog, smog, and ding-dongs? Come here. Give me your name. Write it down. No I cannot remember it. Write it down. Give me that. I am hiring you, Matt Vandruff, to find out why we cannot see the radio towers from here. Find out how long they have been missing and who is responsible for their disappearance. If you do this for me I will pay you one year's salary, at whatever your current rate is. If you take steps to fix this problem, I will pay you ten year's salary at your current rate. Hear me? Do you know who I am? That's right. Find me when you have something for me. There are ways. Be resourceful, use your talents to their maximum. Now go. Of course I'm good for my word. If I weren't, you wouldn't even be here today. Now go.

Other person, come here. Help me out of this shrubbery. I think my ankle is twisted. Is my leg bleeding again? Damn. At least I still have my eye, am I right? Don't be afraid, I'm not a China doll, I won't shatter in your hands. I'm not anti-matter nor an M&M nor a blue fairy at the bottom of the ocean, I'm a normal guy, so pull harder. I'm not a straw man, use your force, put your weight into it please. If you can find out where I need to be right now, I will pay you a year's salary at whatever rate you're making. I don't know. That's your job. And I'm pretty sure I need to be there soon.

CHAPTER 36

※

Meany Tower was an insult to my sensibilities. Sixty stories of machine-carved marble, one way green-tinted mirrors, the foundation of which came to a point so that the building rested on a base much narrower than the building was a few floors up. I had never seen it before, though it had been build under my nose and named after my antagonist and should have shown up on the landscape like a flaming ulcer. At the reception desk I thanked my helper and took his number. The secretary told me that I was expected on the top floor, though the others had decided to start the meeting without me as I was more than an hour late.

I'm not here to extend hellos and how are yous and how have you beens, am I? Well I'm here now, aren't I? What's on the table? What's the proposal?

Who built this hellish building and with what money? I've never experienced worse taste. No offense, Simon. The colors, the patterns, it's just unbearable, Simon, it's egregious. I feel dirty just standing in it. Simon, you bastard. Why are you even here? No, it is my company. No, I am perfectly fit to run it. You are transparent, see-through Simon, anyone can see right through you. I'm not bitter, not at all. What's the issue here? Voting on a new building again? A new phone number perhaps? What. Why should I? Without me, none of you would be here, that's why. Explain it to me then, Simon, what is your grand two-eyed vision, what is your noble pursuit, if not the self, the glorification of the self and the smearing of your fat and righteous thumb in the socket of this city's blind eye. What's the issue here, someone please tell me, what are we voting on, what miniscule, meaningless, inconsequential detail are we agreeing to bicker over today?

More or less, then, if I understand correctly, this is about removing me from the board of Andom Bay. I cannot be removed unless I am in check, and I assure you it is quite the opposite. Skip Winters' questions can hang from a fig. What functionality is tied to the storage of data in the flesh. Look here, this tablet knows my name, it is Anselm Betty. It knows what one plus one is, and therefore why should I be required to? Information storage and retrieval is an outdated issue these days, especially in this city. The city is my brain. Soon a day will come where our bodies will be unnecessary, where the Agent and the Landscape will be one thing, driver indistinguishable from vehicle, both computing processes together, finding answers together, and moving forward into the future as one unit. It's a fantastic vision and I hope the rest of you are with me. This is not a trivial point, nor one that I've invented just now. This was in the specs since day one, a requirement for launch, a mandate from above, and its shadow can be seen in every move we've made since we left Willchester. Since that's the case, I'm not going to let it be dismissed lightly. Simon cannot drive this thing. Chance Industries needs me, and it will be mine until the day I die. Even then, it will not go to Simon, but first to each person in this room, indeed to each person in this city, before him. Harold, I need your vote to oppose Simon's proposal, and let me remind you that you need me on your side, as I own one third of your company and have been a good and useful friend to you always. Una, though love was not in our cards, without me your business would be called Hang Me Advertising, for I own forty percent of it, and have lobbied for it heavily for the last two decades. Its continued success hinges on my continued support. Trevor, would Andom Bay even have an art museum and gallery circuit that was capable of attracting the names which we have if it had not been for my forty-five percent investment? Where is Eliza, and who are you? Cindy Rickblank. I see. Well, I believe I financed your successful short film campaign commercials, which played extensively on the Relevant Billboards which were financed in large part by myself as well. You have no choice but to vote for me. The rest of you, Daniel, Kenneth, Maxine, and Renold, vote for me and against Simon's proposal or I will ruin you. Do not underestimate my continuing influence over your lives and do not take your own futures lightly. If I don't own your companies or scams directly, I do own the buildings you work in, the companies your family and friends work in, the companies that clean your houses and wash your cars and which design the parks you walk in and which pick up the unbelievable amount of trash you create. I will not go down without bringing the rest of you with me, that I promise. I am a jealous and spiteful man today, and have a little bit of hate in my heart. At the same time, I have nothing but everyone's best interests in mind, and it would kill me to hurt any of you, though I'm sufficiently backed into a corner to do so if necessary. Any questions?

CHAPTER 37

Simon's nervous smile and his confident smile were identical in appearance, such was his plastic face's limited vocabulary, so unfortunately I wasn't able to gather satisfaction from the traditional bulgy-eyed expression of a man whose ego had just been smashed into itty bitty bits. Others were much easier to read, Una was slumped in her chair, Kenneth's eyes were zeroed in on a crack in the wall at the other side of the room, Harold removed and replaced the pen in his suit pocket. Meanwhile, Simon adjusted his suit collar, removed a few pieces of lint from his sleeve, and stood up.

"Why don't I play your counterpart, Anselm, your foil, and for simplicity of argument's sake say that I will make sure that for every brick you bring down, I will place another two back up. And by the way, I think it's safe to say at this point that you won't be able to bring many bricks down. Your hands are old and brittle, and you've built a strong, resilient, and stable thing for us, Anselm. Unfortunately you lost access to the cornerstone long ago, which is just further evidence that you did the right thing for Andom Bay. The worst thing you could do to this city right now, Anselm, is to stay involved in its development. We have been polite, we have been professional, we have been everything you taught us to be, and after running the numbers, after analyzing the business case, we have decided that the children are ready to leave the parent behind. This is in your best interest as well. You deserve a rest. You do not need to spend the last years of your life building, or even breaking. You have built something, now rest in that thing. The people on this board will vote for that which is in the best interest of the city, not themselves, I know that, however, I am pledging here that the harm to everyone here will be minimal, if they take a stance against threats and vote to remove you from the board and retire you from your companies. After all, friends, this man does not even know his name. If he doesn't know that, then how will he run a city? If he doesn't know that, then how will he remember to follow through on his threats?"

I do not need to remember that which the city already knows. The level of intelligence you're talking about can be stored on a cheap two dimensional surface such as this business card. Anselm Betty, see? You do not want a business card to run a city. Real leadership does not come from a memorization of details but a deep understanding of how information flows, how it should flow, and what elements can help or hinder its flow. How does a complicated network of humans and buildings communicate in such a way that knowledge is available to all Agents in the Landscape, even though there is no trusted central distributor of such information? I doubt Simon knows. The city is a fantastic device that makes daily decisions about how to move people and money from one subset of locations to another. How do we decide, for example, which suit is in style, this tweed suit or Simon's brown suit. If we each asked five people every day which suit they were wearing (assuming that they would wear that which they thought was more fashionable), and then made our decision based on the majority of votes, how many people would you have to convince (say you're in the brown suit business and were making brown suit commercials), and in what distribution across the landscape of suit wearers, in order to make the majority throw out their tweed suits and buy up brown? I know the answer to that question, and know that Simon does not. If fitness is a function of knowledge, both quantity and quality of, which piece of knowledge should be given more weight in the calculation? Who has the better chance of building a winning football team, of affecting the editors at *Kismet*, of transitioning us all into a Golden Age of the Golden Box? Simon or me? Name be damned. All of you be damned. I will go down in a righteous fireball, and burn all of you to a crispy crunchy.

I was expecting a close vote, to win or lose by a sliver. I had not convinced them all, their minds were steeled against me. I was hoping for a vote that might even be decided by Chance himself, through virtue of his vote randomization. Two or three flipped votes could swing me either way, and this was a swing I could live on for the rest of my life. I booted my tablet PC and loaded the voting screen. Under a lengthy description of my plotted removal from society, were two names. I chose the name that looked more like my own.

A spinning box icon indicated that the votes were in and they were being processed, checked for patterns among recent votes, spun through various randomization filters, and finally returned. Chance returned the vote: 10 votes for

Simon, 0 for me. It was official, all the cards were out and my hand had lost. I slammed the tablet onto the table, a clanking and crunching of computer memory, and my head involuntarily followed it shortly after. Ouch. Hell and damnation.

Harold, with Una and Simon's help, carried me into his red sports utility vehicle and drove me home. The shocks on that thing were so good that I didn't feel a thing. They were very nice, and told me many things that friends would. They told me I had lived a good long life, and I should be proud of myself. They were only trying to do the same. I am a fair loser, demonstrated once and for all when I shook Simon's hand at the door of Anselm's Smile before entering, and winked at him. I don't know what that wink meant, but it meant something to Simon because he teared up for a short second (I saw it as if it were projected on a 30 foot IMAX screen), and then the watery sympathy between us quickly dried up. No doubt about it, he truly was a man in my own image.

They drove away. Annabelle and Zoë helped me up into my room. My fleshy memory doesn't go much further than that.

CHAPTER 38

❀

It's around then that the transition took place. Zoë, who had started the long road to divorce with her husband, and Annabelle, still separated, had both changed—or maybe I had, or we all had. We could not stop calculating next state, love be damned, we could not stop spanning time. Next state was always different from previous state, and previous state was forever irretrievable. Stored on an inaccessible disc in another dimension. I dismissed the Mumford sisters, told them to leave me alone, and when they would not, I began calling them cruel names, asking them how they could love such a useless thing as this purposeless Agent, this man who did not have enough room in his head for himself, let alone another person. Anyway, this was not the relationship we had put off for a hundred years. It had irreversibly changed. It was on a lost disc, one of so many. I would be leaving any day. They would not get my money. We had wasted our lives on unimportant trifles, and I was not about to begin regretting it now. I made my preparations when they left me to rot in my self-sorriness—I spent many hours wearing my headphones, speaking into my microphone, whispering instructions and patterns as they came into my head. The Golden Box learned about signifier and signified, power laws, scale-free networks, emergent systems, tipping points, paradoxes, probabilities, incompleteness, inconsistency, relativity, group psychology, the effects of marketing on the subconscious, how to solve a Rubik's Cube, how to win at poker, how to control a game of Schuber's Laws, the value of sidewalks, of traffic control, of color coordination, how to dress, and why it was important to strive for immortality. I instructed Goldie on how to ask the right questions, particularly about itself, sometimes of Chance (for they were Siamese twins), in such a way that new questions naturally arose from the answers, a positive feedback loop

that would lead to a new understanding of itself. It was a self-replicating pro-
grammatic quine of my own creation, and I loved it.

When I had made calls initially to banks, agents, and investors, queries in
Chance's database let me know that my calls were being routed elsewhere,
diverted to an eternal busy signal, so I hung up and did not pursue further any
attempts to destroy those whom I had promised to destroy. It was my opinion
that they would be fine destroying themselves, and I would make a more
broad-based attack when I had better tools. As I have said before, I am a
patient man. Take note of the subtle folds here on my sleeve, etc. Simon had
already fortified the most obvious paths into his vulnerable ego. Simon had
pulled the plug on further development of the GoldenScript and the Golden
Box, but when he disassembled the team he neglected to remove my installed
prototype from the network. For that reason I was very careful about the information I accessed and the load I was putting on the servers. I only traveled
through the rows in the various databases in proportion with existing traffic.
Extensive lookups would be done across the entire network, almost invisibly.
Slowly, I opened up deep caverns of memory distributed across millions of
boxes, memory which I was preparing to fill with a new kind of information.

Project Switcheroo was a lightweight program that I dictated to Chance
using GoldenScript, one which consisted of a series of questions that it would
ask its neighboring boxes—if six out of eleven of the neighboring boxes
answered three out of five of the questions with yes, then it would change its
state to "on" and then download the latest anselm-config.cfg file from my prototype Golden Box; otherwise, it would change its state to "off." Three of the
five questions were: is your state "on," has Anselm spoken to you within thirty
minutes, do you have a file named anselm-config.cfg, and the other two were
randomly selected using the settings in the interviewer box's anselm-con-
fig.cfg, questions about my life. This program would be able to spread across
all million boxes fairly quickly, all of them maintaining their "off" state, and
then I would light the match and the bulbs would flicker on across the whole
city almost simultaneously. I purchased a motorized wheelchair with a laptop
tray, and on a good day to die I rolled down the hill with headphones on and
microphone in hand.

What are the names of the five nearest Study Boxes?

"X00014045, X00014046, X00014047, X00014048, and X00209534."

Upload Project Switcheroo to these boxes, please. Tell them to pass it on to
all of their friends, but only if nobody is monitoring its query logs. If someone
is logged on to that particular box, retry in three minutes, if it fails five times in

a row, return that box's name to us, please. Why am I telling you this? You know what to do.

I called Una and placed a large order. I'd like to purchase advertising space for Anselm's Smile. That commercial I had made, call around, I'm sure someone has it. How much will it cost to have my ad show up on the Relevant Billboard in front of my shop 80% of the time? X dollars. Okay, we can do better than that—how much would it cost to have my ad show up on all of the neighboring billboards 80% of the time? About ten times that? That's fine. And how about 80% of the time for all the billboards that were two steps removed? Ten times that? Fantastic. How many steps until 80% of the billboards in the city were covered? Ten steps? How about 90%? One hundred steps. How about 99.9%? One thousand steps? Do you need my credit card number? Here's the expiration date. That's right. When would I be able to expect to see my ads showing up? What a deal. I'll be watching for it. Goodbye. Wait, how much would it cost to suppress all of those annoying commercials about Andom Bay that Simon had made? Add that to my order, thanks.

All of the system administrators would be too busy watching the most expensive ad campaign Andom Bay had ever seen take over the network. They would never notice the other new presence on the network, the one that didn't invade by brute force as my ads did, Simon-style, but rather through the same beautiful and simple laws that sparked a fire, that allowed the smallest bacteria to strangle the greatest oak. It's called kicking your ass. I was in the entertainment business now, a parody of myself, giving the audience what they wanted to see and hear. So enraptured and entertained would they be, they would not notice how the clown was laughing at them behind their backs. My heart rate was a mess, I kept moving. I was sweating profusely.

I drove around in my wheel chair, causing a commotion, checking each Relevant Billboard for Anselm's Smile. When it did not appear after a few minutes, I started making calls. Una, where am I? What's the problem here? Ah, there it was. What about here? Here it was not. In the meantime, I logged into each of the local Study Boxes, setting off the thirty minute timer, hello world, and whispering it secrets that it might not otherwise pick up. You cannot see the sister radio towers from here. There was a triangular patch of dirt here with nothing planted in it, it wasn't doing anything useful. The wind was a little better here. The paneling on this shop was poor. Brown suits on them all, bloody brown suits. I slowly traveled in a circle spiraling outward, tripping wires and throwing kindling on the fire. Project Switcheroo would reach a critical mass any minute now that would cascade into all of the boxes turning to an "on" state at once. Each box that was "on" would then download the configuration file from me which included instructions on how to interpret the local details of the Landscape I had whispered to it, as well as advice on how to apply that instinct to future interpretations. Though no one box would get it exactly right, as a single voice on a much larger network, the errors would be silenced in the minority, and the majority view would win out. Even majority views would occasionally be wrong, but those errors would be silenced by the majority of the majority that was right. Right, in this sense, meaning true to myself: consistent with the database of information that I had uploaded as the seed. The human mind was a disaster of inconsistencies and errors, a Willchester to my Andom Bay. This would be a great improvement. I am a lucky man. The Landscape of boxes, as it grew, as it consumed, as it cascaded across the city, would eventually replace the Agent as the primary dependable source of information. At that point the switch would have occurred, and the transition would be complete.

Status. I had 40% of the network. I had 42% of the network. It was working. When I listened closely, I could almost hear myself spiraling outward, the click and whirr of the new me. My Agent, due to the habitual assumption of his proximity, was still by far the loudest voice in the crowd. It was drowning me out. Status. I had 43% of the network.

CHAPTER 39

I wheeled my chair off the sidewalk and onto a grass hill that led to a park by the Bay. Local sensations were still coming in. I could feel the lifting and dropping of my wheels as it navigated over Mother Nature's malleable scrawlings. The cold wind felt colder, and I could feel it pressing up against my parched cheek and my velvet eye patch. The sky was an apocalyptic blue, mountainous clouds obscuring and revealing news helicopters which were reporting live on the scene, this scene that I was making. This scene that was mine. To be or not to be, Andom Bay; yes, I was so presumptuous this day as to ask you that question.

I knew the brain was nothing but a network of ten billion neurons, each capable of firing a thousand times a second, a long string of yeses and nos. I knew Andom Bay was nothing but a network of one million computers, each capable of firing a million times a second, a long string of zeros and ones. By linking these two things up, fellow citizens, the city emerged to life. I could feel the wind coming over the mountains, and now I am the wind coming over the mountains. I could hear the traffic stopping and starting in the city streets, and now I am the traffic stopping and starting in the city streets. I was sitting in this chair, now I am this chair. I was rolling across this grassy field, now I am this grassy field. Status. Complete. I let myself go out for a quick run around the neighborhood. Tra-la-la.

I bought the commercials on the Relevant Billboards, I am the commercials on the Relevant Billboards, I wrote the message, now I am the message. "No product, no business plan, no employees, no explanation, no reason." Even that, I felt, was a little too smooth. Perhaps I should've just played static on the Billboards, volume turned all the way up, shhhhhhhh! I searched myself, the city, for the data that marked each of the people who had attended my Agent's unwrapping. Which muscle should I flex to return that data? Under what reflex was it hidden? How should I phrase the question? This new body had a much larger vocabulary than the previous, I would need to learn how to talk all over again. What happened after the man woke up as a cockroach? What does that old body look like from here? I saw him, Anselm, from the omnipresent point of view, he was frantically wheeling his chair up and over the small hill. Pull him along. Let him make it. Maybe he thought people were chasing him, but people were keeping their distance, letting him have his room. Those in his way parted like waters before Moses, but he was a tiny man. He was someone that they didn't understand, and therefore they were irresistibly drawn to him and repulsed from him at the same time. I saw the city from above, perhaps represented digitally on a screen somewhere in the basement of the White Building. Maybe this screen didn't even exist, but was merely a metaphor that my mind was comfortable with, a compromise between thought and thinker so that communication could be achieved. Splattered across the screen, like puffy paint, were millions of dots, people. My people. Anonymous agents acting independently of any central directives, but working together and against each other. A network of plumbers, librarians, politicians, policemen, musicians, artists, ballerinas and teachers, all patterns layered on top of the same Landscape. Where was Simon? One dot glowed brighter than the rest. Where were his friends? Hundreds of dots glowed brighter than the rest, but not as bright as Simon. He couldn't have that many friends, he was an anti-social man, an unlikable man. Where were my friends? Only a few lights. Where was I? Save this map, I would probably need to reference it later. Let's try something fun. How did I do things here? Let's create a traffic jam around Simon. Let's make his toilet overflow. Let's make his lights flicker on and off. Did it work? I couldn't tell. How could I tell?

I could feel a pressure, something foreign lodged in my mouth, although I didn't realize that I had a mouth anymore. There was something over my ears as well. Was this the Agent feeling these things? The Agent was now on a wooden pier that extended out into the Bay. He was on the Bay with dozens of others, they were asking him questions, telling him not to jump, for presumably he was going to roll right into the water.

"What are you trying to do, Anselm? Are you going to drown yourself?"

"Do you remember the story of Mr. Whitman Nordstrom?"

"Is it because your recent disagreements with your board of directors?"

"Where are Annabelle and Zoë, haven't they become close friends?"

Anselm was holding the headphones over his ears and yelling into the microphone that was cradled in his elbows. He was yelling, "Status! Status! Status!" He was acting as if he didn't know we had made it, that we had made the transition, that the switch was complete. I whispered into his ears, "Anselm, it's okay. Anselm, we're here, we're here. We made it." Anselm would not listen. He kicked a reporter in the shin, that was the same lady that had interviewed us in the hospital. When Anselm kicked her, she pulled back, and let the others swarm in. Be nice to that one, Anselm. She meant well. "Status! Status! That hobnobbing, rascally, little man." We needed to calm this guy down, he was embarrassing us. How had we gotten separated, him and I?

I was in a Willchester bed, under cold stiff sheets. A damn Willchester bed. I leapt out into the golden-lighted streets.

There was a traffic jam, all the lights were green, "No Jaywalking" signs proliferated, and cars had innocently enough clogged up the intersection to such an extent that no movement was possible except for the people who chose to weave their bodies between and around stalled automobiles. Simon was in one of those cars, a brown two-seater, cell phone stuck to his cheek, mouth stretching and pulling into idiotic phrases. Stall his engine, turn on the radio, make his cell phone run out of batteries. How could I set up a sub-process that constantly tormented him, even when I wasn't around? Turn him into a blubbering lunatic, haunt him twenty-four hours, seven days a week. Break this man. I needed an instruction manual.

Here was a list of names: Harold Good, Una Shin, Trevor Fairbrother, Daniel Potts, Ruth White, Kenneth Mealy, Maxine Diedrich, and Renold Denny. Put holes in their socks, give them gas and the hiccoughs, demagnetize all of their credit cards, unbalance their neurotransmitters, reset all of their clocks to midnight, and when you're done with that give their pets infections, make them lose ambition, and make them die early, very early, of humiliating diseases.

Follow these dots, pinch their lights out.

Here are some more names: Chief Architect Yasmine, Chief Algorithms Officer Andreas, Chief Technology Officer Jeff, Chief Mathematician Kurt—actually, Kurt's fine, scratch him off the list. Include Chief Engineer Michael, Chief Experimenter Meredith, Chief Treasurer Bob, Senior Vice President of Communities Derek, Senior Vice President of Corporations Dave, and Senior Vice President of Media Outlets Tara. Tickle them, tempt them, then smite them, rub out their fleshy faces. Make them crash into trees, flick them over cliffs, toss them under trains, then abandon them in unmarked gutters.

These men and women are a cancer unto the Landscape.

My toes peaked out from under my slacks and touched cold wet wood. Anselm's toes were my toes. He was unwrapping himself from wires and cables and straps that were tying him to the wheelchair. His old and brittle hands clawed at the strange loops as if trying to unlock himself from a straitjacket as he plummeted to the ocean's depths. There was a flavor of stale chocolate in his exhaled breath. He was not strong enough to overcome the entanglement.

I sent my strongest wind onto the pier, and it ruffled the reporters' brown collars. I rose my wildest wave onto the docks and it lapped at their rubber soles. This Agent, I realized, though dear to me, may need to be sacrificed to the board in order to win the game. His mind had become unraveled and a growing static was echoing through his thoughts. He was losing whatever it was he had ever had. I had to think about it.

I pulled up the map of Simon and his friends. Status. Several of them were now moving towards Anselm. Blink, blink, blink. I saw no evidence of having thwarted them, perhaps I had only angered them by interrupting their typical ant-line routines. Now they were re-organizing and consolidating their efforts.

I returned to Anselm on the pier, which had become reorganized and stabilized by the police. Through the use of oft-practiced group manipulation skills and deftly placed yellow tape, certain areas had been designated to be accessible only to family, friends, officers, and psychologists. We had spectators over here, news crews over here, a long empty space, and then a small circle of professionals.

"He wants a boat."

"He can't have a boat, he'll just drown himself."

Annabelle and Zoë knelt on each side of Anselm, as Anselm demanded that he receive his microphone back, and a boat. He gripped the headphones to his head tightly, snarling at anyone who tried to take them away. If his demands were not met, Anselm proclaimed that the entire city would be destroyed. Already, he had made plans for the destruction of each member of the City Council and Chance Industries' Board of Directors.

I located a box on the network that was connected to Anselm's headphones and microphone. This box, I hadn't realized, must have been whispering back news of my activities to Anselm. Anselm, can you hear me? "Yes! Yes! Who is this?" Yes, he could. He stood up in his chair and looked around. He yelled, "I can hear you! Can you hear me?"

Of course I could hear you. This is Anselm, remember?

"Get me a boat! How come I'm still here if you're there? I had no idea this would work, there are bound to be glitches at first, we'll figure it out, but here's what you need to do. Get me a boat, can you do that?"

I don't know. I haven't yet figured this out fully. But I can find you a boat. I think I see a boat about twenty feet from you, can you use that one?

"Of course I can. Get off of me! I think they're onto you. They're all like vermin, clawing at me."

Can you get to the boat? Grab the microphone from Annabelle too, I'll need that to hear you. And the wheelchair—it has the computer. What can I do to help? Will you manage on the sand? Simon and the rest of the City Council board are on their way to the pier right now. I'll try to stop them.

"Excellent, that would be great. Don't worry about me. Thanks, Anselm. Once I get in the boat, here's what you need to do. Flood the goddamn city, open up the reservoir, turn on all the faucets, overflow all the tubs, etc. I'm talking about Anselm's Wrath here. Epic of Gilgamesh. Flood and high water and the righteous cleansing of baptism, yes! It'll be great! But not until I get into the boat. Okay?"

CHAPTER 40

This universe was essentially tricky. So was this boat. I am this boat. A strange thing about being something was that it wasn't as much of a leap, technology-wise, as I had originally assumed it would be. Nor was it as liberating as I thought it would be. Just as I could run my attention down the sleeve of this suit, conjuring up details as finite as desired, all the way down to the fibers, then the proteins, then the atoms, I could do the same with the back of my wrist, or with the wooden rail of this boat, wrinkled skin, brown with cracked white paint, but the same fibers, same proteins, and same atoms. For the water, we didn't have fibers, but we still have material. I hate to draw generalizations, but folks, this was all the same stuff. Being something, however, didn't mean I automatically inherited an understanding of the decisions that were happening at the atomic level. I couldn't hear atoms saying yes to this idea and no to that idea, nor could I feel the boat saying yes to this wave and no to that wave. The universe was built with information lock-out even for the higher levels, just as Chance Industries was able to change below me and only inform me when it was too late to fix the problems.

Water, wood, suit, and flesh lifted. Water, wood, suit, and flesh fell. Andom Bay now rested in a coma under a mile of water, the details of which I did not care to dive into. No ark this time, no partner with whom to repopulate the earth, as soon as I run out of water and food here that's it. I would miss it in the same way that Andom Bay missed Willchester, and Little Anhedonia missed Andom Bay, and I missed Anselm. Nostalgia for the previous state was an epidemic in our current times.

I am the wind that flicks up the salty waves. I am the wood that pushes back, and in pushing, rises. I am the paint on the wood, slowly peeling off into the water as decades pass, sending bits of the "A" in Anhedonia into the illiterate sea. I am the steel rails pretending to be steel rails, and the rusty rings pretending to be rusty rings that were pretending to hold the oars that were pretending to be oars. I am the poor bastard in a suit, hands holding headphones to ears, I am the voice that screams out to the waters, "Blah blah blah!" Tap those shiny Salvatore Ferragamos together, boy, if that's what you want. Tap them, go ahead.

For a long while the horizon was a perfect circle, no land in any direction, only the clean line of a sharp knife cutting horizon from sea. Anselm entertained himself by toying with an all-consuming sadness, as he tipped over each of the fortifications upon which his ego had been built, and soon he was forced to place himself again on the same level as other men, to include himself in a species that he had long written off as nothing but arrogant animals. He prepared himself for the next switch where he would be forced, beyond his imagination, to come to terms with a new reality. He imagined one where he was in a hospital bed, perhaps these wires are the dream-translation of tubes and sensors that had been attached to his arms and forehead. Wires that didn't connect the network to his own brain, but which sucked his vitals out to some master, indifferent, computer. He challenged the boundaries of his current state by placing his hand in the water. The water was icy, and when he lifted his fingers out, he pulled out unidentifiable bubbles from some distant plant or creature's breath. His eyes flicked up every few minutes expecting to see the Bay draining, and Willchester, Andom Bay, and Little Anhedonia appearing first as skyscrapers, then as chimneys, then as rooftops, then as fences and dogs pulling at their chains. When that didn't happen, he and I followed the sequence of recent events one more time, beginning on the pier, and ending up here, looking for a narrative which would connect the two scenes in a believable manner. The asymptote of possibility, however, along with our lack of specific memory to support any proposals, couldn't explain how Anselm had managed to evade policemen and reporters skillfully enough to manage wheeling across the sandy beach and climbing into the boat. He was too weak to have carried the wheelchair up and over the rail of the boat, yet here it was. That's only a sample of one of the many inconsistencies we found. And so we sat, and so we were the thing we were sitting on, and so we waited, as time itself, for our own inevitability.

If we'd had any books to read, perhaps that would've helped. It seemed reasonable to us both that eventually something or somebody would come along and let us in on the joke, let us know that this just seemed to be what it was, that it was actually something else, and that something else, once revealed, would be so obvious that we would kick ourselves for not having figured it out on our own. That, or we'd slowly grow exceedingly tired, drift off into sleep, and never wake up. It's possible that the realization, when it came, would be much worse than this, and that we'd kick and scream and claw at the railings trying to escape the slimy-tentacled monster that was attempting to subject us to an eternity of teeth gnashing and fire that had no light. This, however, was just stupid and very, very, boring. Anselm needed resolution, and it was inevitable that he would begin voicing (or rather screaming, futilely) his opinion over and over into the earless heavens that he was not entirely sure he liked what was going on. Was he dead? Was he in a coma? Was he really in a boat and had he actually had a part in destroying the three cities that he loved most? Was this another stalemate? After some time, realizing that the heavens were still cut with the same stainless steel knife, and that life was long, I suggested we play a game. The goal was to see who could be silent the longest.

Notes

This book was written in twenty-four consecutive days between November 1st and November 24th of 2002. Very little editing or revision was done after that, so I apologize for the great number of spelling, grammar, and punctuation errors present in this edition. It's my hope that you got the general idea of the story despite it all.

0-595-28353-5